FRIENDS WHO LIE

PAUL J. TEAGUE

ALSO BY PAUL J. TEAGUE

Don't Tell Meg Trilogy

Book 1 - Don't Tell Meg

Book 2 - The Murder Place

Book 3 - The Forgotten Children

Standalone Thrillers

Dead of Night

One Last Chance

No More Secrets

So Many Lies

Two Years After

Now You See Her

Morecambe Bay Trilogy

Book 1 - Left For Dead

Book 2 - Circle of Lies

Book 3 - Truth Be Told

PROLOGUE

Benidorm: June

AS MURDERS GO, it was a beautiful place to die. There were two of them at the top of the hill. Both had started their day with different intentions. For one, events took a sudden and violent turn. For the other, a day that was full of promise ended before it had even begun, with a blow to the head, followed by a desperate struggle, and then strangulation.

The Benidorm Cross was one of the best known tourist spots in the area and was often featured on TV in holiday shows and drama series. It perched high on the hill overlooking the resort, its glorious golden beach and the sparkling blue seas of the Mediterranean.

There was no way anyone else in the group would make that climb before they had to pack up for the flight back home. Sure, they'd all said that they might when the Cross was pointed out to them in the distance. It was a challenge, goading them from the beach and the bars, always whispering in their ear: *Will you do it? Can you do it?* But, when push came to shove, the arduous walk had been too much effort when set against the lure of the bars, the beach and the vibrant nightlife.

They had both made their way out of the apartment block alone in the early hours of the morning, leaving their lightweight companions sleeping, tired and hungover from the previous night. What a night it had been, too. A time to heal the wounds of the big bust-up of the day before. It had been cathartic. They'd needed it to blow away the resentments and friction, to make a fresh start.

At five o'clock precisely, the mobile phone had vibrated under the pillow, its owner already awake, plotting, planning, working through every scenario. They all had the motivation to commit the murder, that was for sure. That's if the finger was even pointed at the group of friends. The police would probably think it was some hobo or opportunist. That's how it would look. The others would still be in bed while it was happening – the body would be discovered before they'd even opened their eyes.

Just after six o'clock a second mobile phone alarm had vibrated and was immediately switched off. There would be no shower, no breakfast. An immediate start should mean avoiding any other tourists. There was always the danger of the early morning dog walkers, but so high up on the hill? Unless they lived in one of the walled houses that lined the winding road to the Cross, that seemed unlikely.

The streets were quiet at that time. The late-night revellers were not that long home and in their beds, while the early starters wouldn't get served breakfast in their hotels before half-past six. The resort's thoroughfares were getting the only two hours' respite from noise and shouting they got in any twenty-four hour period.

The mobile phone map indicated the route. It was straightforward, a short walk along the seafront, then the road began to rise, a warning of the climb to come. There was not a person to be seen. Benidorm was wonderful like this, but you had to be an early bird to catch this stillness. The road became steeper and more difficult to tackle, to either side residential properties taking the place of hotels. On foot it was a long slog, but at least the sun was not in its midday intensity, there was still a coolness to the air.

It was necessary to pause from time to time – the incline was relentless. The concrete blocks which lined the now single-track road provided an ideal resting place. The scenery became rockier, the vegetation sparser, but the higher the climb, the greater was the promise of the views from the top. All was quiet. Not a dog walker to be seen, no cars raced by on the narrowing road making an early morning dash to the top.

Eventually the road came to an end. There was a parking area there, but no vehicles anywhere and no sign of anybody else. Perfect, this was perfect. The others would miss it all, wasting the last day in their beds sleeping off the night before. This was the ideal antidote to the rowing and bickering, and then the drunken hilarity of the reconciliation afterwards. It was a place to think.

The climb was more gradual at this final stage, a dirt track lined with rough wooden fencing marking the way to the large metal cross mounted on its concrete plinth. It was nothing special up close. But there was so much of interest up there, before you even stopped to admire the views. The Cross was surrounded by memorials to people who'd visited Benidorm and cherished their time there. There were photos of loved ones with messages saying how important this place had been for them.

In memory of Mum, she adored this resort and now she can enjoy it forever xxx

To Tom, from your Benidorm boozing mates. We had great times here. We miss you pal, The Wigan Crew

There must have been fifty memorials surrounding the Cross – artificial flowers, teddy bears, photographs – many of them held down by stones to prevent the hilltop winds from blowing them away. Somebody had even left an urn of ashes on the concrete plinth.

The light wooden fencing marked the limits of the viewing area. The panorama was stunning. The sun glistened on the gentle waves below, the sands were golden and bright, and in the distance was the black rock of Peacock Island. The high-rise hotels and tacky bars merged into a harmonious architectural vista which it was easy to miss out on when submerged in the energy and noise on the streets below. It was a wonderful view of a much maligned resort. To be there alone, at an early hour and at such a quiet time, was a real treat.

The killer was concealed among the clusters of bushes, alert, nervous but determined; from their safe spot, they too admired the magnificent views that the hilltop afforded. They should have walked up there together really, but it was too late for that now. It was too late for many things.

As the second visitor arrived at the hilltop, they saw that it would be easy enough to duck under the fence and walk to the edge of the summit. There were memorials out there as well, so it had to be safe enough to step out a little further. There was no cliff edge, it was free from danger.

The memorials were touching in their simplicity and sincerity. In many ways they showed a more acute sense of loss than any grave could ever convey.

To Grandma and Grandpa. We had so many lovely

Christmases here with you. We miss you both so much, but we know you're still laughing in heaven. Dave, Lorna and kids xxx

Toni. We loved this place together. I'll always love you. Mike.

It took a moment to realise what was happening: a rustle to the side ... a sudden movement ... a sickening blow to the head ... a fall to the ground ... blood running down the face. Before there was time to recover, a second blow, hard and violent. What was this? *Who* was it?

There was a struggle to stay conscious, then a moment of darkness followed by the full brightness of the sun in their eyes.

A face, at last a face. Who was doing this? Then, a third, violent blow to the forehead and the sensation of fading away. Why was this happening? The moment of realisation. This person was known, it was no stranger. This was no random attack.

There was a final surge of energy, a last attempt to escape and perhaps even to reason. But then the hands came down around the neck and the squeezing began. It was almost finished; their victim was growing weaker.

The killer would always remember those last, choked words as the body weakened and death finally came. It was slower than expected, it took some time to die. The area was checked for silly mistakes. No water bottle left behind, nothing with fingerprints. The assassin rolled the corpse into the undergrowth, then swept the surrounding area with a branch from one of the nearby bushes to remove any sign of footprints.

It was still early – there was nobody else to be seen. The killer rapidly walked down the hill, clinging to the walls of the houses beside the road, alert to anybody who may have been looking out of windows or taking in the delights of the new day from their balcony.

All was quiet as the murderer walked through the empty Spanish streets and headed back to the apartment. Nobody was awake. They would not even be aware that somebody was missing, not until nine o'clock at least. That left plenty of time to reflect on the victim's last, plaintive words: 'I thought you were my friend.'

ONE

Caitlen: April

CAITLEN CURSED TERRY, and not for the first time that week. His careless, happy-go-lucky demeanour was wearing thin. Another night late back from work. Another night eating dinner on her own. She was beginning to wonder if she'd even notice the difference without him. Only she was scared of being on her own again.

She sifted through the post which had been thrust through the letterbox after they'd left for work. She wanted kids eventually, but after the day she'd just had she wondered what life would be like with them. She was tired out from a terrible day, hungry – with no inclination to cook – and in desperate need of a good night's sleep. Terry's snoring was becoming a problem, too. Intermittent had become regular, it was keeping her awake at night.

The post was non-existent most days. They'd gone paperless with the bills, so that had culled most of what they received. Nobody wrote letters any more, meaning that anything they did get was just a pile of crap. Unwanted circulars seemed to be all that was keeping the Royal Mail in business.

Caitlen looked in the fridge. The problem with them both being out at work all day was that they never shopped properly. It was a constant process of grabbing bits on the move. Terry was no use. He always seemed to remember his beers, but never milk, bread, eggs, or anything else which might have kept the two of them alive.

She looked at the clock on the cooker. Just after six-thirty. She was starving. Anything they did have in the house needed some preparation, and she couldn't be bothered.

Her phone vibrated. It was a text from Terry.

Sorry luv, going to be held up until after ten. Big case, you know how it is. See you later.

Three years ago, the word 'luv' had been novel and even slightly endearing. The way Terry said it there wasn't a hint of being patronising. It was just how he and his family spoke. Now it grated like a toddler's screams, it was an assault to her ears. She winced every time he said it. It was only a matter of time, but it was so hard for her to jump off the moving vehicle. Life kept moving on, jumping out of a relationship took grit. Caitlen wasn't sure that she had it. And with Terry, it wouldn't be easy.

His text had sealed the deal. She'd go to the new bistro that had opened up the road. It would still be happy hour – she could grab a pizza and a glass of wine and they wouldn't worry about her using her laptop in there. It was one of those cool places run by hipsters. Caitlen checked herself out in the mirror. She looked tired, but perfectly alright to be seen in public. A change of jacket, a brush of the hair and she'd be good to go.

She reached out to pick up her MacBook, but then hesitated. Her old laptop was sitting on the kitchen worktop where it had been getting in the way for some time. It was ready to be thrown out, but she wanted to check over the hard drive first and make sure there was nothing on there that she needed. Nobody was getting her information from an old hard drive and stealing her identity, she knew the drill. Then she'd pound the thing to bits using Terry's mallet from the shed. Terry was the kind of man who kept a mallet. He had a toolbox, too. He even had a workbench. Only dads use workbenches in the twenty-first century, she'd thought to herself.

His hands were rough and dry, toughened from doing jobs around the house. Caitlen wasn't used to men who were practical. Most of her previous boyfriends would have struggled to put up a curtain rail. She missed the touch of their soft hands. When Terry caressed her, the callouses on his palms scraped her skin. It was the little things that drove her crazy.

She placed her MacBook on the kitchen table and picked up the laptop, opening the lid and switching it on. It was half-charged, enough for her to do what she needed to do without it dying on her. She'd kill two birds with one stone, check the computer and get a bite to eat. It was beginning to look like a night she could get enthusiastic about. If things went really well, Terry would be back after she'd gone to bed and she could play dead, avoiding the need to engage with him. He'd feel guilty, so he'd try not to wake her. And she could postpone biting the bullet for another day.

Caitlen knew that she had to end things with Terry. But it was so disruptive. She'd moved into his house and rented out her small terrace. She'd have to coincide the break-up with the end of the tenancy agreement so that she'd have somewhere to live. And she still wasn't completely certain that she wanted to end things. She was mid-thirties and beginning to wonder if she'd ever meet the right man. Her ovaries wouldn't stay ripe forever. She'd even considered using Terry, then leaving him and taking the child. Naomi and Rhett made her realise what she was missing. They always seemed so good together. They were a proper couple.

The bistro was just what she needed. Being happy hour, it was pleasantly full. There was a work party on the big table in the corner, but the waiter considerately placed her on one of the small tables some distance away from them. There was another guy working on a tablet two tables along from her, a couple in earnest conversation to the other side, and other small groups dotted about creating a nice hubbub of conversation so as not to make her feel too self-conscious.

The guy who was sitting on his own looked up and checked her out as she was shown to her table. She noticed it and glanced back at him. Soft hands, she thought to herself. She had to break it off with Terry, but not that way. For all his faults, he was good to her most of the time and he still made her laugh. Maybe that's why she was still around. Nobody had ever made her laugh like Terry. Even if he was an idiot, he knew how to tell a joke.

'I'll try a vegan pizza,' she said to the waiter. He had a beard like she'd never seen before. Its end hovered just above his notepad as he scribbled down her order. 'And a small glass of red wine, please. Do you have Wi-Fi?'

He pointed out the password at the bottom of the menu and walked off to pour her glass of wine. As soon as she'd taken the first sip, Caitlen relaxed. She'd done the right thing – this was just what she needed. It had been a tough day at work. The new boss was a prize bitch. Caitlen had often wondered about going it alone, but she was as scared of leaving her job as she was of leaving Terry.

She took out her laptop and placed it on the table. She forgot her password at first – the constant array of secret words that were needed to navigate modern life sometimes got the better of her. At last, she was in. As Windows finally booted into life the jingle announcing the device was ready to go sounded out loudly, causing the hubbub to stop momentarily. The laptop's speaker hadn't been disabled.

'Sorry,' she said, her face reddening.

The man with the soft hands looked up and smiled.

'Don't you just love Windows computers?' he said. She could tell he was educated. Terry was a graduate of the university of life, as he'd proudly announce: 'Those idiots in their black gowns and letters after their names can't teach me anything that would have ever been useful in my life. University is a waste of time!'

Caitlen smiled at the man. He was obviously putting out feelers. No wedding ring either. Would it matter for one night?

'Yes, sorry about that. I haven't used this one for some time, I'll switch the speaker off.'

They looked at each other – it hung in the air, but she chickened out and went back to her computer. She wasn't that kind of girl, although the way things had been recently she was seriously tempted.

She set to work on her hard drive, immediately unaware of what was going on around her. It was always like this for Caitlen. She loved working with computers and did what Terry casually dismissed as 'geeky stuff' for a living. She was a software programmer and had a great aptitude for the work. She would become immersed in the lines of code and had loved it until the bitch arrived. When Dick retired and sold the business, the atmosphere had changed. It was the only job she'd ever had. Thirteen years in the same workplace, that had to be worth a gold watch.

Caitlen checked the files on the hard drive. Most of what she did was in the cloud, safe and sound. But when she'd bought the laptop, cloud storage had been expensive, so sometimes she kept private stuff in folders she made hidden in the settings. It was those she wanted to check out.

There were a couple of useful things that she spotted straightaway. There was an old savings account from university days that she'd completely forgotten about. It might have a couple of hundred pounds left in it. She transferred the account information to her password manager, she'd check the balance later.

Another folder had some photos of her and an old boyfriend. She'd loved being with Euan, but he hadn't liked her enough to stick around.

She angled the laptop towards her, to be certain that the man wouldn't see it. As the waiter approached with her pizza, she moved her things away from the place mat.

Eager to tuck into her pizza, Caitlen scanned the hard drive files for the final time. She was about to slam down the lid when she spotted a folder with an unusual name: BTC2011. What was that? She double-clicked and took a look. Inside was a text file containing two strings of very long passwords.

Then it came back to her. Christmas 2011. Stuck in the office with one of her mates – though Luke was a bit more than a mate back then – killing time before they could go home and start the seasonal celebrations. An afternoon of doing no work and surfing the internet for interesting things to do. And an expenditure of a hundred dollars which she'd completely forgotten about.

What was in that folder would test her friendships, change her life and result in a vicious murder.

Caitlen didn't get to try her first vegan pizza that night. And the hopeful young man seated to her side didn't get lucky.

TWO

Caitlen: April

KEEPING her secret for that week had been exhilarating. And now here were her best friends sitting around the table, chatting away, completely oblivious to what she was about to tell them.

Caitlen had rushed home from the bistro, almost neglecting to pay her bill, and completely forgetting the young guy who'd been looking at her expectantly as she got up to leave. The waiter sporting the extraordinary beard had been concerned that they'd somehow frightened off a new customer and she'd had to tell a lie to shake him off.

'My youngest child is ill, that's the babysitter. I'm so sorry. I have to go.'

She handed him a twenty-pound note, which would more than cover the bill, and rushed home. She couldn't wait to fire up her MacBook. If she was right and she could figure out how to use those passwords correctly, this could change her life.

She *was* right. Caitlen wanted to scream at the heavens with joy. She'd thought nothing of it when they were playing around at their desks in 2011. She'd had to think hard about the hundred dollar cost at the time, it being Christmas. But Luke had convinced her to do it. And now her life was about to change.

There was a small round of applause, shaking her out of her distraction.

'Sorry, I was miles away, what did you say?'

'We're engaged, it's official, look!'

Becky held up her ring. She was glowing with happiness, delighted to be sharing the news with her friends.

But there was somebody at the table who wasn't quite so delighted to hear the announcement. Caitlen looked at Harriet who was spinning her wine glass round by its stem, looking intently at its contents as they swirled up and down with the circular movement. Matt looked uncomfortable, too. Becky should have picked her moment more carefully, but she was like that. Insensitive and careless. She probably hadn't given a second's thought as to how it would make Harriet feel.

Caitlen seized the moment. She allowed the congratulations to be passed around, the hugs, the whoops and the kisses. Then she struck, before everybody's attention went back to their small huddles of conversation.

'I've got some news of my own to share.'

'Oh yes? You didn't tell me. Don't say I'm going to be a father!' teased Terry.

She hadn't told him because she still wasn't sure how he fitted into her plans. He was a technical idiot, hopeless with computers. He knew enough to find car websites and tool suppliers, other than that he was clueless. That suited

Caitlen. They weren't married, this didn't have to involve Terry. She'd figure that bit out afterwards.

Everybody was watching her. No one had expected an announcement from Caitlen, yet it was true that on the conveyor belt of meeting, dating and living together she and Terry were now at the fork. Next came marriage or children. Nobody thought a break-up would be coming. Terry was far too much fun.

As she surveyed her friends' faces, Caitlen let them guess. She could see their minds whirring. Baby or marriage, take your pick. Well, surprise! It was neither.

'Before you all start trying to guess, it's not a baby and it's not a wedding. It's something completely different.'

She saw a look of relief cross Terry's face, but he was quickly in there with a quip.

'Thank heavens!' he said. 'I just put our life savings on the 3.30 at Cheltenham ... and the bad news it's now 8 o'clock and I lost the lot!'

There was polite laughter, then all gazes turned back to Caitlen.

'Oh no, it's not bad news is it?' Emmy asked. 'You haven't got cancer or anything, have you?'

'No, no, it's nothing like that. It's good news. And it involves all of you, my best friends.'

There was a collective sigh of relief.

'In 2011, well before I'd even met Terry, I was at work just before Christmas with an ... an old colleague of mine, Luke Chester. He's left the country now, gone abroad, but we always used to get on well. Very well, in fact.'

In front of her sitting next to Emmy, Porter took a slow sip of wine, settling in for the story.

'You know what it's like when you're killing time in the office in the run-up to Christmas. You have to be there, but everybody else has packed up early and gone home. We didn't have anything to do, so we were just messing about online--'

'Don't tell me you found my porn videos?' Terry piped up.

Everybody laughed.

'No, this has nothing to do with video nasties, Terry!' she sparred back, keeping things light.

'You've all heard about bitcoin, yes?'

There were mutters around the table. They'd all heard about it, with the exception of Terry who made some terrible joke about half-eaten chocolate coins in his Christmas stocking. It fell flat. The consensus was they'd heard of bitcoin, but hadn't got a clue what it was.

'Well, in 2011 even fewer people knew about it and it was really complicated to buy. So that afternoon Luke and I set ourselves a challenge. The first one to find out how to buy bitcoin didn't have to make the next cup of tea. That was it. But it kept us both occupied all afternoon.'

'Did you find out how to do it?' Rhett said, wishing his wife Naomi had been able to make it to the meal to hear the news.

'Luke did,' Caitlen smiled, 'and I had to make the next cup of tea. I'd completely forgotten about it until I checked my old computer last week. But I've still got the bitcoin I bought on that day.'

Terry was clueless as to what she was suggesting, but their other guests had cottoned on straightaway. They'd seen the sneering news reports about millennials who'd paid off their university fees with cryptocurrency and lucky couples who'd invested tiny amounts years ago and were now millionaires.

'My goodness, how much is it worth now?' said Kasey.

He was a fellow geek, he and Caitlen often bonded over web code. He understood exactly what she was saying. Even Terry had shut up now. He hadn't got a clue what they were talking about but he could see Caitlen had the undivided attention of the room. Anything capable of usurping Becky's engagement announcement had to be worth listening to.

'It's worth over half a million dollars now … give or take a few thousand.'

There were gasps around the table. Terry's face went white.

'What's that in pounds?' Emmy asked, ever the journalist.

'Four hundred thousand or thereabouts, depending on the exchange rate.'

'Damn it, Caitlen! What are you going to do with it?' said Becky, who'd now completely forgotten about her own engagement.

'That's why I need to speak to all of you. I can't take it all out at once. I've only managed to get fifteen thousand out so far.'

'You didn't tell me about this,' Terry said, no longer in his usual upbeat voice. 'When were you going to tell me?'

Caitlen ignored him and carried on.

'The truth is, I'm terrified it will get stolen. I can't keep it on an old laptop, it's like keeping your life savings under the mattress. People can just hack this stuff and help themselves.'

'Can't you stick it in a safe?' Rhett asked.

'It doesn't work like that. I'll need to convert it into money I can spend, and I can't do that all at once. It's not like traditional banks.'

'I can't believe it,' Harriet said, the first words she'd uttered since Becky's announcement.

'What will you do?' Kasey asked.

'That's why I need your help. I'm petrified someone is going to steal my bitcoin. I need to keep it safe until I can figure out what to do with it. I've managed to move it onto a small device – it's like a USB drive, but very secure. It's as safe as it can be there, but only if I don't lose it or it doesn't get stolen. The device is protected by a recovery password, a list of twenty-four random words. They keep my half-million dollars safe and secure: that's all that stands between my newfound wealth and a Russian hacker.'

'And what do you want from us?' Emmy asked, sensing the big reveal was on its way.

'I want to share two secret words with each of you. You're the only people I trust. You'll each get two of my passwords and I want you to remember them, that's the securest way to store this information. It's the only way to make sure nobody steals my bitcoin. Is everybody okay with that?'

'So you want us to remember two words each, is that right? Can we write them down?'

'No, you mustn't write them down. Nobody can do anything to get the bitcoin unless they have all twenty-four words and I'll keep hold of the last eight. I'd trust you all with my life, so I know that I can rely on you for this. It won't be for more than a month, two months at the most.'

'What about me?' Terry asked.

Caitlen stumbled in her reply.

'Well, er, don't worry. I'll keep our eight words in my head. Even I can remember that many words. Everybody alright to do that?'

There were nods around the table. Terry looked as if he'd just been excluded from a private members' club.

'Thank you! I knew you'd help. I know it sounds paranoid, but hackers steal this stuff all the time. By the way, to say thank you I'm taking us all out for a treat. How does a week in Benidorm sound? I'll foot the entire bill.'

THREE

Naomi and Rhett: May

'YOU STINK OF BURGERS!' Rhett said, the minute she placed the kiss on his cheek.

'And you smell of red wine, so you obviously had a better evening than I did.'

'How was it?'

Rhett didn't really want to hear the answer. He knew how it was. Smelly, noisy and unpleasant. Still, it would be his turn at six o'clock the next day.

'We had a group of teenagers in causing trouble. They were having a food fight across the dining area. It caused a right mess. Little buggers were out of there by the time the police arrived – in fact, we'd almost got the place cleared up by the time the police arrived. I'm sure they time their arrival so they have to do the least work possible.'

'As good as that? Well, the minimum wage pay packet will make it all worthwhile. By the way, I got an extra shift first thing tomorrow morning. Three hours, six until nine o'clock. I'll be back at my desk by nine-thirty ready for our meeting with Ted Maxwell. It's another twenty-five pounds in the kitty. It all helps.'

'How much longer do we need to keep this up, Rhett? I mean, seriously?'

She stepped out of her uniform. She was wearing the Victoria's Secret underwear that he'd bought her in better times. What a waste of great undies, in a fast-food restaurant of all places. She looked gorgeous, but Rhett knew better than to make a move after a long shift dealing with spotty teenagers. All she'd want to do is sleep.

'We just need to land another contract. Just one bite and we'll be in the clear. If Maxwell signs with us, we can both quit. It'll buy us the time we need.'

Naomi was undressed now, her uniform neatly folded on a chair and her underwear discarded at the top of the pile in the clothes basket. He could see how the long shifts on her feet for hours on end were taking it out of her. Both of them were better suited to lighter work. Graphic design to be precise. Their idea of the perfect working day was spending eight hours at a MacBook Pro, sipping filter coffee, Coldplay on in the background and messing about with some colour palette in Photoshop. It was money for old rope. But Rhett had got careless, and he would forever be in Naomi's debt for taking it on the chin.

'Anything from the lawyers?' she asked, as if reading his mind. 'Or the insurance people, come to that?'

There had been a letter from the lawyers and it hadn't been good news. He wasn't sure whether to tell her or not. She'd put on her dressing gown and was getting ready for a night-time shower.

'It could be as much as five thousand pounds.'

He watched the sharp intake of breath.

'Bloody hell, Rhett. Why did you have to cut corners like that? You know the rules as well as I do. It's ended up costing us more than it would have if you'd just paid for the image properly.'

She'd taken it on the chin but that didn't mean she wasn't furious with him. How could he have been so stupid? They'd learned all about copyright law at university. They'd been in the same classes together, although it had taken some months until they became a couple. They'd bonded over a Pantone colour chart.

'They're still pushing for full recompense. Five thousand pounds for swiping a single image. And what about the insurance? Have they said if they'll pay up?'

That was her fault. It was probably why she'd taken the moonlighting shifts so well. Naomi was in charge of the paperwork, that was the deal. When they'd gone it alone as Crossley Graphical Solutions, just the two of them, they'd divided up the work. She was in charge of the professional indemnity cover. Only she'd let it slip for a month, waiting for a new contract to come in before paying the bill. And now they were in a dispute about whether the insurance company would pay up or not. It was in the grey area that insurance companies seem to love so much. She was as much to blame as he was.

'We're never going to get out of this loop, Rhett. How long is it going to take us to pay off that five thousand pounds? It's going to take a lot of burger flipping to even make a dent in it. And if the insurance doesn't pay, we'll have the legal expenses too.'

She was crying now. She couldn't discuss the issue without becoming emotional about it. Rhett put his head in his hands. It was bad, he knew that. Once word had got round that he'd used an image that wasn't free of copyright, a couple of clients had got the jitters. It had needed damage control – at least Naomi was great at that. Most of the people they were dealing with were grey-haired men of a certain age, every one of them clogging up the glass ceiling in their executive roles. Rhett was grateful at times for their old-fashioned attitudes. They loved to deal with his extremely attractive wife and it meant that they still had a handful of contracts left. But none of it was enough to pay the mortgage.

'I hid from an old school friend this evening. The shame of it. I was mopping the floors and I recognised her voice. She didn't even look at me, but can you believe it? I actually hid in the broom cupboard until she'd eaten up her burger and gone. I couldn't face her seeing me there. It's only a matter of time until our friends find out. Or, even worse, Caitlen. I'd die if she ever discovered what's happened.'

'They'll find out eventually. If we end up paying a fine, it'll probably make the local paper. And you know what Emmy's like, she never misses a trick. In fact, it'll probably be Emmy who ends up writing the story for the newspaper.'

Naomi was sitting on the side of the bed. She didn't look at Rhett, she was talking to herself as much as to him.

'I just feel so ashamed. To be caught cheating and then being so daft as not to have insurance. And what if we lose the house? I know it's petty, but I've always felt the need to be better than Caitlen. It goes back to when we were kids. I love her, but it feels like we were in a race with each other since the day we were old enough to care. It's just so embarrassing.'

'If I were you, I'd start playing nice with your sister. She had some interesting news at the meal this evening.'

That made Naomi look up.

'You told them I had a headache, yes? Did they fall for it?'

'Of course they did. They all sent their love. Just make sure you stick to the story and we'll be fine.'

'Great. So what was Caitlen's news? She hasn't said anything on Facebook.'

'She's come into some money,' Rhett began. He watched Naomi's face go white. There was always this one-upmanship thing between them, he never understood it.

'How? There is no money in our family. If there was, I'd be doing my best to get my hands on it.'

Rhett explained the situation.

'Can we even go to Benidorm with them? Can we afford the time away from our horrible little teenager jobs? We could earn an extra two hundred pounds taking extra shifts in that time. How on earth has she managed to make herself that much money? Bitcoin, did you say? I thought that was some kind of scam.'

'It's no scam – it's for real apparently. And I thought the same as you about the time we're going to lose. But she's giving us all seven hundred euros to spend over the week, and all our expenses are paid for. If we bring the laptops, sneak in some contract work and hold some of the money back, we might be able to get a free holiday and even end up better off.'

'Did she say anything about splitting the money? With family, I mean.'

'No. The general feeling seemed to be that she's buying us all a free holiday and that's as far as it goes. We're really lucky that she even thought of us. Besides, I don't think she knows what she's doing herself yet. It's complicated, as far as I can tell. It's not like normal money. You can't just take it out of your bank account and spend it.'

'Do you think she'd help us out? If she's got all that money now, what would we need ... ten thousand? To pay the fine, the lawyers and catch up with the mortgage--'

'Naomi, take a breath. She's only just found out herself. It's a lot of money, I know, but it's not so much that you can go handing it out to everybody with a begging bowl. Ten thousand is a big dint in that cash. It's quite an ask. And could you bring yourself to ask your little sister for a handout?'

Naomi was silent. She was thinking things through.

'We might have to. Damn. It's so humiliating this, having no money. I hate it. This fine could sink us, Rhett. It's serious. If Caitlen's got her hands on some free cash, that could be our way out of this. I'm going to call her.'

'It's past eleven o'clock, you can't call her now. And certainly not to ask her for cash. I'd play it cool if I were you. Everybody at that little dinner party will have a hundred and one uses for Caitlen's money. Let's just go to Benidorm and take it from there. We can maybe work on her together, let her know the fix we're in.'

Naomi had a face like thunder.

'She's always been like this, Caitlen. She always gets the luck. I work my arse off in the business and get nothing and she pisses around at work and ends up making half a million dollars. I love my little sister but at times she makes me so furious. She gets all the breaks. Sometimes I wish she hadn't been born, it would make my life so much easier.'

FOUR

Benidorm: June

'YOU CAN'T KNOCK that for a flight, even if it was a budget airline!'

Caitlen felt great. It was amazing to be able to pay for a group of friends to take the trip out to Spain. She'd felt invigorated the moment she'd handed in her notice to the bitch. She was already getting a taste of what it was like to have a bit of money, especially when it had been magicked out of thin air. To be able to access all that cash without having to earn it was an incredible sensation for her.

The hot air had wafted over them as they stepped out of the plane onto the asphalt at Alicante airport. They'd left behind the dreary grey skies of the UK and were all ready for sunshine and sand.

'How far is it to Benidorm from here?' asked Porter. 'I don't know about you, but after that terrible weather we left behind I'd be happy to sit here on the runway for the week. This sun is glorious!'

'Everybody got their passports?' Becky asked.

'You sound like my mum!' Emmy teased.

Becky looked as if she'd been scolded. Emmy was a bit blunt like that, but she hadn't meant anything by the comment. Becky could be over-sensitive at times. Nobody knew that more than her new fiancé Matt, who was doing his best to carefully steer her away from Harriet. There was a tense truce between the two women, and it was fragile to say the least.

'Come on, guys!' Caitlen chivvied. 'The sooner we get through customs, the quicker we can jump on the shuttle bus and check into the apartments.'

She felt every bit the hostess on this trip – she'd thought of everything and paid for the lot. Her budget had been ten thousand pounds, although she'd done it for less. She'd actually paid in cash, handing over the notes to the travel agent. The look on that girl's face! Caitlen liked having money. She knew she wasn't rich in a Mark Cuban or Richard Branson kind of way, but it was exhilarating to be able to spend that amount of money in one sitting, knowing there was more to replace it.

In the intervening weeks, Caitlen had withdrawn another twenty-five thousand pounds. She'd now got just over thirty thousand sitting in her bank account. That would do her for a year. She'd figure out what to do with the rest. It was so much money, she didn't even trust the bank with it. She was petrified of losing it all.

She'd placed another three thousand pounds in her joint account with Terry. They'd always kept their own bank accounts as a legacy of their single days and each month they'd transfer over their share of Terry's mortgage, the bills and the food budget. She'd been deliberately evasive with Terry about how much she was taking out.

'I've got enough money to cover the holiday and to give us a bit of a boost in the household budget. We'll be able to treat ourselves whenever we want to now, without giving it a second thought.'

She'd hoped it would placate Terry, at least in the short term. It didn't. He wouldn't stop worrying over the issue of her money. It was as if he sensed it might not be coming his way.

'It'll be nice if we can get the mortgage paid off early. I might be able to think about changing my job,' he said.

The day Terry changed his job, there would be Spanish sunshine across the whole of the UK for thirty days in a row – it was as unlikely as that. He was married to the force. It allowed him a certain freedom in his relationship – the unsociable hours, the erratic nature of investigations. It was very easy to lose time if he wanted to.

'Yes, it's quite exciting to think what that amount of money could do,' Caitlen replied.

She avoided mentioning Terry and the cash in the same sentence. It was always referred to in the third person, but never specifically in plans that might have included him.

The passport queue took some time to go down. They'd introduced an automated system and the older generation simply couldn't cope with its demands. Caitlen watched as an old lady placed her passport three different ways until she finally figured out the correct orientation. She wanted to cry sometimes. Terry was like that, useless with technology. It was as if it just passed some people by, their brains couldn't cope with it. For Caitlen, it was the most intuitive thing on earth.

'Did you see that old bird?'

A man was chuckling behind her in the queue. He'd

been friendly on the plane too, when she'd walked along the aisle to use the toilet.

She turned around. He had a broad smile. His skin was tanned golden brown and he had a deep, silky voice. His shoulders were incredibly broad, as if he worked out. Caitlen smiled. Terry was up ahead, playing the jester with Emmy, Kasey and Porter.

'Did you see her? I know she's old, but really ... If you sent somebody through with a blindfold they'd have made a better job of it.'

The man laughed. It was wonderfully rich and warm, he had an easy charm.

'Wesley Nolasco,' he said, holding out his hand. 'Call me Wes. Pleased to meet you. Are you here on your own?'

It occurred to Caitlen that one day soon she could be. Alone. It was easy to meet new people. Perhaps she could make it without Terry.

'No, I'm with a group of friends. How about you?'

Terry was fooling around ahead of them. He'd messed up the passport machine – in fact, he seemed to be making more of a pig's ear of it than the old woman. The poor security guard who was there to help the British tourists navigate their way through the automated devices looked as if she was dreaming of the days when a grumpy guy at passport control would coolly take your passport directly from your hand, pretend to scrutinise you and your photo, then wave you through as though he'd done you a big favour.

'Travelling alone,' he replied. 'Just how I like it. Where are you staying? I haven't got my digs sorted out yet. I don't know this area very well. I'm heading for Benidorm.'

'Us too,' Caitlen replied. Normally she'd have been more protective about her information, but she was with a big group of friends. What could possibly go wrong?

'Amazing!' he beamed back at her.

What an easy charm compared to the forced jollity of Terry. It had taken her a while to see that. Terry's eyes seldom gleamed when he told a joke. It was the laughter that was more important to him. He liked an audience.

'How are you getting there? I was going to jump in a taxi, but that's quite expensive. I do bar work and music stuff when I travel. I like to keep things cheap.'

'We've booked a shuttle bus, it works out really well in a group. Do you have luggage to pick up?'

'Just my guitar, they won't let me bring on my instrument as hand luggage.'

He turned to the side to show Caitlen the rucksack that was strapped to his back. Wesley seemed to travel very light.

'I play in bars sometimes. It saves me from having to get a proper job. Benidorm is full of pubs and clubs and packed with Brits. I'm hoping that somebody will pay me to play covers. That way I can stick around for a couple of months.'

The queue shuffled forward, it was almost Caitlen's turn. She looked ahead, trying to figure out which way round to hold her passport.

'That's wonderful, I'd love to be able to play an instrument. Being a musician is like being a hairdresser. You can make money wherever you go and people always want your services. So long as you can play well, that is.'

Wes laughed. What a smile he had.

'Can I hitch a ride in your bus? Is there room? I'll pay my way. It'll work out cheaper than a taxi. I take it you're heading for the centre – you haven't booked somewhere rural?'

The money was making Caitlen more reckless than she might have been normally. Day-to-day life meant planning for the worst, covering the downside and always thinking ahead. Well, from where she was standing, ahead was looking pretty darn good.

She thought for a minute. Kasey had ended up with his own apartment. Harriet had been up for sharing with him, but she figured that it would be nice for them to have some privacy. Would Wesley be alright sharing with a gay guy? He looked like he'd be cool, not the macho type. He was a musician, after all, not the sort of man that Terry was. She truly believed that Terry didn't care that Kasey was gay, but he just couldn't leave it alone. He'd always make quips if they went to the bathroom together. Ridiculous and old school. Kasey was the straightest gay guy she'd ever known. She never even thought about it.

Caitlen decided to keep quiet about the room going spare in Kasey's apartment. She'd see how Wes fitted in with the others first. But she liked him. She felt that Wes might inject a new dynamic into the holiday. He looked like he was a man with interesting stories to tell.

'It's my turn with the passport. Look, jump in our shuttle bus, there will be several seats spare, I booked a big one. That's my group standing together on the other side of the machines. Come and join us when you've scanned your passport. And don't worry, the bus is paid for. Have this trip on me!'

Wesley touched her on the back as she moved towards the machine. She thought that odd, but forgot it immediately as she placed her passport into the device and it gave a churlish electronic sound of rejection. She turned it around, annoyed that she'd messed it up. She looked into the screen, holding as still as possible so that it could scan her eyes. It messed up again. The Spanish security guard intervened and set Caitlen right. Her face reddened, she'd made more of a mess of it than the old lady. Eventually, the barrier opened and she was on her way.

Wesley had already made himself known to the group. They were all teasing Caitlen after rejoicing in her struggle to get through passport control. Wesley looked as if he'd always been part of their crowd. Already, he'd slotted himself in like and was chatting to everybody like he'd known them for years.

FIVE

Benidorm: June

IN SPITE of the general enthusiasm for the trip, the heat got to the travellers straightaway and they were pleased that the shuttle bus was waiting for them in the airport parking bays with the air conditioning set to super cool. The driver seemed relieved that he wasn't transporting a party of drunken Englishmen.

'We're carrying one extra,' Caitlen said, as Wes waited at the bottom the steps, expectant that permission to board would be granted.

Caitlen was grateful that the driver was Scottish. She didn't speak Spanish and had studied French at school.

'You've paid fer the whole bus, lassie!' he announced. 'You can bring yer entire family fer all I care. Hop on board, son. Yer welcome.'

Wes moved to the back of the bus. He was getting on really well with Kasey. She hadn't even considered that their new recruit might himself be gay – he seemed to be sending out all the right signals in her direction. Maybe he was bisexual. Caitlen checked herself, cursing the way Terry's comments had worn her down over the years. But it was good that the two men seemed to like each other. Maybe Kasey would suggest the room of his own accord, he might see it as welcome company. It was only for a week – it would give Wes some time to find a place of his own. It seemed harmless enough.

Caitlen stood at the front of the bus making sure they were all on board. It wasn't lost on her that the way they were seated told its own story. Kasey and Wes were chatting away at the back of the bus. Wes was touching Kasey's arm as they spoke. Maybe he was just a touchy-feely kind of guy. Emmy was talking across the aisle to Terry, with Porter next to her looking out of the window, like a spare part in their conversation. Emmy and Terry got on well. She was a journalist on the local paper and he was a detective sergeant. Their jobs often brought them together, either on a crime scene or at the receiving end of a press request for a statement or a comment. They'd known each other before the friendship groups moved into the same orbit. In fact, Emmy and Porter were the common elements. Caitlen knew Porter, Emmy knew Terry, and that's where their less than beautiful love story began.

Naomi had been sour-faced since she'd learned about the money. Caitlen had expected her to be pleased for her, but as usual Naomi just couldn't find it within herself to be happy for her younger sister. Caitlen had almost considered removing her from the guest list, but she liked Rhett and didn't want to cause a scene over it. Naomi might have had a little more grace about accepting the invitation. It was as if she thought it was the least Caitlen could do.

Naomi was deliberately avoiding Caitlen's gaze, no

doubt cursing her sister for surveying her kingdom – a cheap shuttle bus heading for a Spanish resort. Harriet was sitting alone at the back, well away from Becky and Matt who were at the front, next to Rhett and Naomi. Perhaps they were hoping that some of Naomi's marital bliss might rub off on them. She'd done well with Rhett, he was a good-looking guy. They'd been together forever. They'd met at university and had set up their own business, whereas Caitlen had drifted between relationships and lasted longer in her job than she had with any man. And now she was stuck with Terry. Naomi had done much better in life than she had.

Caitlen moved past Terry, who barely acknowledged her, and sat next to Harriet. She seemed grateful for the company.

'Sorry Harriet, it must be difficult at times with all these couples.'

She realised what she'd just said.

'Sorry. Again. I know it's tricky for you with Matt here. I haven't really had a chance to talk to you since the meal. Are you okay?'

Harriet looked stoic.

'I'm fine, Cait. You know how it is. He liked it so he put a ring on it. What can I do about it?'

'But it came out of nowhere, didn't it? Am I the only one who thinks that was a bit fast?'

'You know what Matt's like. He's the marrying kind. We only separated because I asked him to cool it. I mean, I love ... I loved him, he's a great guy. But it was too fast for me. Becky seems to be lapping it up, though.'

'I don't think I've ever seen anybody who was so proud to be engaged. Have you seen the size of that ring? I like

Becky, but she can be hard work sometimes. I hope Matt doesn't live to regret it.'

Harriet looked as if she was about to say something, but stopped and looked out of the window. They were moving now.

'This place looks amazing, Cait. Thanks so much for treating us like this. I couldn't have afforded it on my own. I'm really grateful.'

'It's fine, Harriet. I love being able to do it. You're my friends and I am making you earn it, after all. You can still remember your two passwords, I take it?'

'Don't worry, I won't forget them. It's a crazy way to keep your money safe, I've never seen anything like it. Where do you keep the actual cash – or bitcoin – or what-ever it is you've got?'

'That's just it. I'm geeky and even I struggle to get my head around this stuff. It's all stored on a secure device which is ... er ... let's just say it's safely stored where nobody will find it. All I've got to do is not die between now and when we move the funds over. Hopefully I can manage that. I know some people say Benidorm is a bit rough, but I think I'll make it to the end of the week, don't you?'

They laughed. The countryside was becoming hillier and more rural, every now and then they'd catch a glimpse of the sea sparkling in the sunshine. The lack of greenery and the burned soil hinted strongly at a week of excellent weather.

'I certainly hope so!' Harriet smiled. 'Did you give Terry anything to remember? He seems a bit put out about the whole thing.'

Caitlen felt her face reddening. Had she been that obvi-ous? She lowered her voice.

'Can you keep a secret, Harriet?'

'Of course I can.'

'Seriously? You and I have known each other forever. I trust you as much as my sister, even if she does walk around with a face like she just sucked on a lemon.'

'Yes, Cait. I won't tell anybody.'

Caitlen lowered her voice even more.

'I'm not sure if this is going to involve Terry. I think this might trigger the end of the line.'

'Oh Cait, I'm sorry.'

'It's okay, it's been brewing for some time – well before the money came along. It's not that I hate him, I just feel like we're done. Like it was a just a three-year thing. It's run its course, I think.'

'I'm sorry, Cait. Terry always seems so much fun to be with.'

As if on cue, Terry let out a loud guffaw. Wes looked up, startled. He returned to his conversation with Kasey.

'It gets a bit wearing after a while. You can have too much of a good thing. I'm going to see how things work out on this break. I want to give it a chance, but I honestly think it's over. Getting this money means I can move on cleanly.'

'Will you give him any of it?' Harriet asked. Perhaps she should have been the journalist, rather than Emmy.

Caitlen's face gave her the answer. Terry was going to see very little of the money.

'I'll keep my mouth shut,' Harriet said, squeezing her friend's hand. 'I hope you're alright. I just want you to do what makes you happy.'

'You too,' Caitlen replied, grateful for the unconditional support. She'd already sensed the change in attitude towards her among her friends. Only Kasey and Harriet seemed not to care.

'Maybe you'll find a decent bloke out here, you

certainly deserve it after the drought you've been through. I hope it wasn't too obvious giving you an apartment on your own?'

'Of course not, I'm grateful. I wouldn't mind a holiday fling. Something completely casual, that's just what I need at the moment. Do they have Tinder in Spain?'

Caitlen laughed and stood up to walk over to Terry. She was for real about giving it another try. Terry had the week of the holiday to convince her. He didn't know it yet, but he was on his yellow warning. She'd picked up that much from his interminable football games.

The road signs were now indicating that Benidorm was only a few kilometres away and the air of excited anticipation increased. Caitlen's mobile phone began to ring and she looked for a spare seat to sit in.

'Who's this, I wonder?' she said aloud, as she moved along the aisle. She looked at the screen, as she sat down to take the call.

'Oh, it's my money guy!' she announced as she pressed the green button on her phone.

She only just caught the words from the seat in front of her as the voice of her financial adviser came through the speaker.

It was Naomi and she was mocking her sister.

'*It's my financial adviser!*' she sneered. 'Of course it is, Caitlen. Who else would it be?'

SIX

Matt and Harriet: May

'GOOD MORNING, BEAUTIFUL,' Matt said as he opened up his eyes to greet the new day. The love of his life was beside him. If it could be like this forever, he'd be a happy man. But he'd blown it and it was his fault.

Harriet smiled at him. It was just like it had been before. Only, he had to go back to Becky now. He'd have to see it through. He was in too deep.

'Make sure that you text Becky. You know what she's like. She needs to know your every waking move.'

Matt wasn't in the mood for it. He'd managed to sneak off for what Becky thought was a night away on a business trip. It had been hard work. She insisted she'd travel with him when they were married. He was trapped and it was all his own stupid, impetuous fault. If only he'd been more patient with Harriet.

'What time are you in work, Harry?' he asked.

'Ten o'clock, it's the joy of flexitime. Council wages might be terrible but the perks are superb.'

Matt looked at her, the curve of her breasts barely concealed by the sheets. Their clothes were strewn across the floor, the debris from a frantic, passionate encounter. It had been six months. Half a year of tortuous separation, wound licking and posturing. And an unhealthy rebound relationship with Becky who'd always had her eyes on Matt since the day she met him. But Becky was possessive, erratic and demanding. If he tried to paint her in a more sympathetic light, he might have wondered if there was a history of mental illness there. When he'd realised his mistake, she'd threatened to harm herself – she couldn't live without him now, she said. And so he was stuck in a crawl towards a marriage which could only imprison him.

He rested his head on his arm and looked closely at Harriet as she struggled to keep her eyes open. He could hear the sound of her gentle breathing inches away from him. Her long auburn hair rippled over her smooth shoulders, she looked beautiful to him.

What had he been thinking of? He'd been so angry with her when she refused to get engaged. Why hadn't they talked it through?

'I'm so sorry, Harriet,' he said quietly, not for the first time.

She stirred, turning to face him now, the sheet moving below her waist and exposing more of her perfect body. Matt wanted to reach out and touch her, to kiss her neck and immerse himself in her beauty. But they had to talk. This might be the last chance they'd get. Like a persistent outbreak of damp rot, Becky was permeating all elements of his life. This would be his last night away from her – she'd made that clear. It was probably his final time alone with Harriet.

'You were an idiot, Matt. What were you thinking? I know you were angry with me, but we could have talked it through.'

'When you handed me back the ring, and said you weren't ready ... I'd just assumed that you would say yes. I was hurt and confused. I was angry with you. I couldn't understand why you were rejecting me.'

'I wasn't rejecting you, Matt. You know I love you, I always have. But you also know how my dad used to beat my mum. I grew up around that. And when the bastard finally did us all a favour by having a heart attack, she moved a pervert in with us. It just made me nervous about marriage. I was happy as we were. I felt that getting married would jinx everything. And I should have told you, I know that now.'

'I had no idea. Yes, you should have told me. If I'd known what your childhood was like, I'd have waited. I'd have understood why you wanted to take things slow. I can see that you weren't rejecting me, it was those men that you were pushing away. But I'm not like that. You know that, don't you?'

She placed her hand on his face and stroked it gently. They had to talk and plan. This couldn't continue, however much they both desperately wanted it to. Becky was a monster, they'd not even realised that until Matt had begun his relationship with her. In mixed company, she was like anybody else, just a little needier. Behind closed doors she was manipulative and demanding. And now she was Matt's problem.

'You could leave her, you know. It'll be horrible and messy, but eventually things will return to normal.'

'I don't think I have the strength. She's threatened to harm herself more than once. I couldn't live with myself if she did that. I have to go through with it, Harriet. I just wish we'd done this five months ago instead of keeping a polite distance.'

'It's my fault too. When you ran off to Becky, I was furious with you. I know I was cold. But when you made your engagement announcement at Cait's dinner party, I had to have one last try.'

The others had noticed that she'd been silent when Becky made her big announcement. It caught Harriet completely off-guard. She'd assumed that Matt was only using Becky to get back at her, that it would end and they'd start over again. But unknown to everybody else around that table, Matt had become caught up in a deadly trap. In his mind, there was no getting himself out. He'd convinced himself that Becky would have to leave him of her own accord – if she ever did that. He would never be able to leave her, she wouldn't let him.

Harriet had made sure they got a moment in the kitchen alone.

'I'll make the drinks,' she'd announced. 'You sit down, Cait. Enjoy your moment. How many teas and how many coffees?'

She'd looked at Matt directly when she spoke. It was probably the first time their eyes had met since he'd stormed off in a huff. It had been six months of avoidance, evasion and polite greetings at occasional social events. When she looked directly into his eyes, she wondered if they were the only ones that could see the spark that had just shot across the room.

After Harriet had gone to make coffee, Matt gave it a moment, then made an excuse.

'I've changed my mind. Actually, I think I'd prefer a filter coffee. I'll go and tell Harriet.'

He'd stood up to walk through to the kitchen and Becky's hand – the one sporting her new engagement ring – shot up to stop him. Caitlen sensed what was happening and distracted Becky with some wedding talk. Matt sneaked into the kitchen. As he walked up to Harriet, she spun around and they began to kiss. It was deep, passionate and urgent. Their bodies pressed close together, comfortable and familiar in spite of what had happened. Matt pushed Harriet up to the worktop, one hand moving towards her leg. His other hand knocked a cup which went crashing to the floor.

Like an alert guard dog, Becky's voice could be heard calling through from the dining room.

'Everything all right in there?'

'Sorry, Cait, I just dropped one of your mugs!'

Matt moved away, Harriet hopped off the worktop and smoothed her dress. Their faces were red, it was obvious what they'd been doing.

'We have to speak, Matt,' she whispered. 'You can't go ahead with this.'

Even as she said the words, he knew there would be no way out. But he had to see her, one more time. He had to try to tame the fire that Harriet had lit within him.

'I can get away Wednesday. The King's Hotel on Warwick Road. I'll book a room. I'll tell Becky I'm away on business.'

Matt looked behind him to make sure the coast was clear. He kissed Harriet one more time, then made a commotion about heading up the stairs to the bathroom. There was no way he could join them in the dining room, not until he'd had some time to cool down.

And so there they were, sharing a bed together for what was possibly the last time. Matt needed time to stand still, he wanted to be stuck in that moment forever.

'If I'd come into some money like Caitlen, perhaps we could make this all work. We could run away, disappear and never see her again. In many ways I think it would be better for Becky that way, to completely vanish and never be seen again. I think that's the only thing she'd accept.'

'But we don't have Cait's money and we can't just walk away. I have my mum to visit in the home and how would we make a living if we went to another country? I shuffle papers for the council. You're a sales rep, although I suppose that might be useful abroad – if you can find something that you can sell.'

'I hate what I've done. I despise the way she's cornered me like this. If we had that money, we could dig ourselves out of this hole. I could get away from her poison.'

'We don't have her money and we never will, Matt. You've made your bed and you'll have to lie on it now if you're not prepared to end it with her. I know about people like Becky. It can only end in death. Either her death or the death of the person whose life she's ruining. It's how my mum escaped from my dad. If you can't end it now, if you don't have the guts for the fight, you're going to have to see it through to whatever bitter end it comes to. And you and I will have to try our best to walk away from each other.'

Harriet moved closer towards him. He could feel her breath on his face and could wait no longer. He pulled her close into him, his hand touching the small of her back and they made love until Harriet had to leave for work, her face flushed and her hair dishevelled. As Matt watched her walk through the door of the hotel room, he vowed that some way and somehow they would be together again. Whatever power she held over him, Becky had to go. Whatever it took, he was going to be with Harriet.

SEVEN

Benidorm: June

'SORRY, Caitlen, he's insisting that the booking is only for five rooms. Two singles and three doubles. They must have mixed it up.'

Wes was letting her save face. He was the only one who spoke any Spanish, and he was being very generous with his translations. It was Caitlen who had messed up the booking, Apartamentos Tres Torres was full because of a special event that was taking place in the town and somebody was going to have to share a room. The look on Naomi's face told her that at least one member of the party had managed to figure that out for themselves already.

'They're sure they haven't got any more rooms? What about after the weekend? Will people check out then?'

Wes spoke to the man at reception. Caitlen didn't need to understand the words, she picked up on the sentiment.

'He says it's possible, but it's a busy time of year. You've paid for the apartments in full and he says that you can move everybody around as you please.'

Caitlen was too hot. The shuttle bus had been refreshingly cool, but she'd become overheated and sweaty dragging the suitcase along the path up to the entrance of their block. At least it looked nice. There was a lovely pool, the other residents seemed civilised and it had a plush, modern interior. The online blurb had said that it been given a full makeover for the new season and it looked like they'd been telling the truth. It was time to bite the bullet.

'Thanks Wes, I'd better see if we can shuffle these rooms without annoying anybody too much!'

As Caitlen walked over to the group of chatting friends, she ran through the configurations in her head. She thanked her lucky stars that none of them had kids – that would make what she was about to do even more combustible.

'Okay everybody, sorry to keep you waiting. They've messed up the booking, I'm afraid.'

She decided to tell a white lie about that. If Wes was happy to collude with her and maintain an untruth, she would go with the flow.

'Somebody's going to have to share a room. Harriet has a single room with twin beds, so does Kasey. Wes is moving in with Kasey for the week, but Harriet gets to keep her room because everybody else is a couple. Fair enough?'

'If anyone ends up sharing with us, somebody might want to take that spare bed in Harriet's room. Especially once they hear Cait's snoring!'

Terry laughed out loud, making a German couple who were checking in turn around and look at their party. Caitlen was embarrassed to realise that they were probably fearful of getting stuck in an apartment block packed with drunken British louts. She wished that Terry was capable of laughing more quietly.

'That leaves the couples,' she said, ignoring Terry's remark. Nobody would be very enthusiastic after a night sharing an apartment with Terry. She was struggling to remain enthusiastic herself.

'I'm going to suggest that Naomi and Rhett come in with me and Terry. Sorry Naomi, but I think that's fairest, don't you?'

'I don't mind sharing with you and Terry,' Emmy offered. 'We all rub along well enough.'

'Well, Matt and Becky are just engaged, so they're defi-nitely not sharing!' Rhett offered, kindly. 'I say the engaged couple are out of bounds. That's fair, isn't it?'

Becky took Matt's arm and pulled him into her.

'I'll go for that!' she said. 'Thanks, Rhett.'

'At least everybody's on the same floor, they got that right,' Wes said, as he rejoined them from the check-in area, a handful of plastic key cards in his hand. 'So, how are we carving it up?'

Caitlen examined Naomi's face. She looked like she'd just been told she had one week to live. Rhett whispered something in her ear and she perked up.

'Okay, Cait, we'll come in with you and Terry. And if we all get on each other's nerves, I guess we always have spare beds in Emmy's apartment and Harriet's room if anybody needs a bit of space.'

Caitlen was relieved. Her sister could be a bit negative sometimes, but it helped considerably if she didn't make a fuss. Rhett was an easy-going guy and as for she and Naomi – well, they were sisters, they were stuck with each other, they'd figure it out.

Wes handed out the key cards as if he was giving away

the last of his food. They'd been a bit tight with the cards, Caitlen thought, bearing in mind how many of them there were in the party.

'All the apartments should be the same inside, so it doesn't matter who takes which one. And you can swap before we all unpack if you don't like your view!'

They picked up their cases and began to move en masse towards the lifts.

'If I can get an extra apartment after the weekend rush, I will,' Caitlen tried to reassure them.

As far as she could see, that was the best configuration of people. She and Naomi would be fine – they were very different from each other, but they always figured it out. Besides, she needed to speak to Naomi. They'd not had time to talk properly since the meal. There'd been so much going on what with her news and Becky's surprise announcement. They needed to catch up and sharing the apartment would push them together.

There were two lifts serving the apartment block and they had to make the trip in groups of three and four, depending on the sizes of their suitcases. They gathered on the landing of floor five. It was a long, marbled corridor with six doors evenly spaced around the hallway. The single apartments were at either end, which meant the doubles were spaced two along either side. Caitlen felt a pang of anger as she realised that they'd have had a full floor to themselves if she hadn't messed up the booking.

There was a problem with the rooms. Becky was making a fuss.

'I'd really like a sea view if somebody else doesn't mind swapping?'

She let her request hang in the air, awaiting a response.

Caitlen saw the real reason why she wanted to swap

rooms. They were right next to Harriet's apartment. She knew that things were tense between her and Harriet, so she immediately stepped in to help out.

'Take our room!' Caitlen said, a little too quickly. 'You're welcome to it – you are the happy couple, after all.'

Becky's face lit up. Matt looked up the corridor towards Harriet's room, a wistful look on his face.

Terry was on the wrong side of the hallway, clumsily attempting to open up the door to the room which Caitlen should have booked. He gave it a shove, banging his shoulder hard against the wood.

'Damn it, Terry, it's a holiday apartment, not a police bust!' said Rhett. 'We're on the opposite side, mate.'

Terry had made so much noise, it had brought the apartment's occupant to the door. It was a young woman – probably no more than twenty-five years old, Caitlen thought – standing in a bikini. Terry's jaw almost hit the floor, Porter turned to gawp, and Rhett, as a man who was accomplished at staying married, took a crafty peek then looked back at his wife.

'Hi, is everything alright?' she asked.

'It just got better!' Terry said. He was sounding more and more like a 1970s comedy act by the day.

'I'm sorry,' Caitlen intervened, moving towards the woman and indicating that Terry should step out of the way. 'We got our rooms mixed up, sorry to disturb you.'

'So, you're my new neighbours.'

'Yes, we are. And I promise we won't always cause this much disturbance. We've just fouled up the room bookings and we're trying to figure out who goes where.'

'It's no trouble, honestly. It was a bit quiet up here, to tell you the truth. It'll be nice to hear other people coming and going.'

Terry had started to move their cases into the opposite apartment, encouraged by Naomi and Rhett who wanted to get in and unpacked. Becky and Matt also went into their room, eager to get showered and changed.

'I'm Gina Saloman, pleased to meet you.'

'Caitlen Brinkley. That's my ... my partner, Terry. Sorry, he can be a bit of a fright sometimes.'

Gina laughed.

'It's fine. How long are you here for?'

'Just the week. And you?'

'Oh, I'm here for the summer, probably much longer than that. I live and work out here, I can't stand the weather in the UK. All I need is a laptop and a wireless connection and I'm good to go. I was just heading to the pool, it's wonderful down there when the weather is like this. I'll see you around, you'll love it here, the apartments are fabulous.'

For a moment, Caitlen felt a pang of envy. It was a craving for a new and freer life, like the one Gina was leading. She worked in software, all she needed was a laptop and an internet connection, just like Gina. The only thing that was stopping her from dropping everything and moving somewhere nice like Spain was Terry. He was her biggest encumbrance. He was her only block now that she had the money. As Gina smiled at her, pulled her door shut and walked confidently along the hallway with the boldness that only a twenty-something could enjoy, Caitlen decided that she wanted to be Gina Saloman. She wanted her life to be just like hers.

EIGHT

Benidorm: June

AT LEAST CAITLEN had managed to get something right. The apartments were fresh, modern, clean and beautifully furnished.

'No minibar, though!' Terry had said, after searching the kitchen and lounge as if it was some forensic examination.

'It's an apartment block, that's why,' Caitlen replied, still preoccupied with the stunning Gina Saloman. She could hardly blame the men for gawping. She was amazing. Terry, meanwhile, seemed unchanged by the wonderful environment in which they were now immersed.

'All we need is a fridge full of John Smiths beer and we're away!' he said conspiratorially to Rhett.

'There's bound to be a British supermarket close by,' Rhett suggested. Naomi was frequently antagonised by Terry's behaviour – she'd made herself scarce, feigning another headache. At least they had separate bedrooms. Terry had made a fuss about the twin beds.

'They're getting pushed together!' he'd declared. 'There's no way I'm spending a week on holiday and being miles apart from Caitlen in the bedroom. What is it with the Spanish and their separate beds? It's a wonder any of them stay married.'

Caitlen would have preferred a single bed in a separate room. She was anxious to speak to Gina and find out more about her lifestyle. She wondered if she'd be able to sneak away to the pool and join her new friend. She didn't want Terry in tow when they spoke next. His bad habits seemed accentuated abroad. She was finding him more and more embarrassing.

'I'm going out to find some beers. Are you coming, Rhett?'

Rhett nodded, thinking it was probably the course of least resistance. Besides, he was anxious to get a look at the beach. He was certain that once Terry had got his precious John Smiths beer, he'd be amenable to reroute along the beach. Caitlen was grateful for the headspace once they'd shut the door. She'd just realised how little time she and Terry had spent together in recent months.

Naomi was out of the bedroom the moment the two men had gone.

'I thought you had a headache, Naomi?' Caitlen said.

'No, just a pain in the butt.'

Naomi looked at Caitlen and they burst out laughing. Whatever the tensions between them, they were still sisters. They could always make each other laugh, even when they were fed up with each other.

'He can be a bit much, can't he?'

'You're saying! I don't know how you've put up with

him as long as you have. I mean, he doesn't really fit in, does he? With our group, I mean?'

Caitlen's immediate response was to challenge Naomi. She might have done six months ago. There was no love lost between Naomi and Terry. He thought that Rhett was emasculated by her. Only, 'emasculated' was not a word that was in Terry's vocabulary. He'd put it slightly more offensively than that. *If you carry on like this, she'll turn you into a Kasey!* Naomi had told Caitlen she'd wanted to punch his lights out at that, not only because of how he thought she was some kind of evil agent who was eroding Rhett's inherent masculinity, but more because of his attitude to Kasey. The man was a copper. What chance did the public stand if attitudes like that were so deeply ingrained?

There was little point arguing with Terry.

'That smells like the stench of prejudice, Terry,' she'd dared to challenge.

He passed wind loudly and offensively.

'That smells like the stench of yesterday's dinner!' he replied.

And with that crass behaviour, everything stayed as it had always been. Terry would casually allude to Kasey's sexuality in his coarse humour, the others would write it off as 'Just Terry being Terry.'

'Can you keep a secret?' Caitlen asked. 'You mustn't even discuss it with Rhett. Promise?'

'Of course!' Naomi replied.

'I'm thinking of leaving Terry.'

She'd said it. It felt daring, scary and exhilarating.

'Seriously?' Naomi asked.

'Yes, I'm serious. I should have done it before we came out here. I wanted to give him a chance, to see if it was just me being stupid, but he's an idiot, isn't he? I can't believe it's taken me so long to see it. You all know that already, don't you?'

Naomi didn't say anything. They all tolerated Terry. It wasn't that they didn't get on with him, he could be a great laugh at times. But he wore you down. He needed to be something else in the modern world and he seemed incapable of making the change.

'When will you do it?'

Caitlen noticed that Naomi wasn't questioning her decision. It seemed her sister was several steps ahead of her when it came to Terry.

'If your mind is made up, you shouldn't wait too long. It will only make things worse.'

'I don't want to screw up the holiday for everybody, but I can't stand the thought of him being close to me. You heard what he said about the twin beds. And he wheezes when he's been on the beer ...'

Caitlen began to cry. She'd been holding it all in, not daring to articulate her thoughts in such detail. Her earlier chat on the bus with Harriet had been sounding things out. Now she was talking specifics, not generalities.

Naomi hugged Caitlen. They hadn't been so close in a long time. Naomi looked like she wanted to say something too, but she held it back, allowing Caitlen to speak.

'I'm going to see how easily I can outmanoeuvre him while we're here. He'll spend most of the holiday drunk, and if I'm lucky he'll fall asleep before he gets any ideas. There's always Harriet's apartment too, if I need a spare bed.'

Caitlen dabbed her eyes with a tissue. She wasn't the crying kind, but breaking up with Terry scared her. The money would complicate things.

'How do you think he'll take it?' Naomi asked.

'Badly. He must know it's coming. We're like strangers in the house. He must have noticed, however busy he is at work.'

'There was life before Terry, you know. You've split up with boyfriends before. There will be a life after Terry.'

'Yes, but the money is going to make things difficult. He's going to think that's what this is all about. I come into some money and he thinks he's going to be able to get his hands on it. Then I tell him to sling his hook. How would you like it if you thought you were going to get some of that cash and I told you to take a hike?'

That question was a little too close for comfort for Naomi. But Caitlen was dead right. If Terry thought he was getting a half share of all that cash, then immediately got dumped, he'd be furious. It would be like thinking he'd won that week's lottery only to find he was looking at the numbers on an old ticket. Incredible elation followed by devastating disappointment. It would be enough to drive even a sane person to murder.

NINE

Terry and Emmy: May

'IT'S one heck of a lot of cash, even if it is Monopoly money,' Terry said, sitting up in the bed and revealing a chest that was dense with thick black hair. For Terry, the idea of waxing or even grooming was something that only youngsters did. A hairy chest had worked for Sean Connery and it had also worked for Terry all of his life.

'Still, if I could get my hands on my half, we'd be well away.'

'Has she said anything yet?' Emmy asked. 'When will it hit your joint account?'

Emmy looked like she'd just had the night that she'd just had. Her long blonde hair was matted and messy, the remnants of her make-up smudged.

'You look like one of those paintings from that artist guy ... what's his name ... Picasso. Everything is there, but it's not quite in the right place.'

Emmy didn't mind Terry's humour. In fact, she loved

Terry. The only person blocking them from being a couple was Caitlen. They'd been planning to tell her and Porter after the dinner party, but Caitlen had messed it up by mentioning the money. And now they had to park their plan for a little longer, so that they could figure out what to do.

Terry's mobile phone beeped at the side of the bed. He quickly read the message.

'It's Cait wondering how the surveillance went. Better not tell her that it was highly satisfactory, eh? And that I got to see way more than I bargained for?'

Emmy blushed a little, but only for a moment. The thought of she and Porter ever pushing the boat out and trying something exotic in bed was unthinkable. It was like having sex with a comatose man. It always felt as if he was putting himself through an endurance event and one in which he was not doing very well. Terry was fun, in bed and out of it. They shared the same coarse humour. She didn't know how she'd ended up with Porter, he was an idiot.

'Does she really not suspect you, Terry?' Emmy asked, checking the time on her phone. 'She's not stupid, she must at least have an inkling of what's going on.'

'I think she's just pleased if I leave her alone when I come home. If I come on to her, she pushes me away, so I try it on more and more, because while she's saying no to me it diverts her from what we're doing.'

'I feel terrible doing this, Terry, but it's only a matter of time. She must feel the break-up coming. I just worry what will happen to the group when everybody finds out. They'll have to take sides.'

'I don't think it'll be like that, Ems. I think she'll be pleased to get rid of me, especially with this bitcoin thing or whatever it's called. We just need to hang on a bit longer to get our share.'

'Just think, I'll be shot of Porter, you'll get rid of Caitlen and we'll have cash in the bank. We should take a year out, you know. We'll both be able to get sabbaticals from work.'

'Yeah, I love that idea. My lovely Emmy all to myself and no crooks and criminals to chase for a whole year. We can spend the days sleeping in and going to the pub. Sounds like journalist and police heaven to me.'

'Have you got your hands on any of the money yet?'

'Only a small amount. She keeps going on about how it's not like proper money and you can't just get it out of a cash till. She's moved some over into the joint account, but I think she's got lots stashed in her own account. She's keeping it deliberately quiet, I reckon.'

'We need to make some progress when we're in Benidorm. I'll talk to the others, see if I can get them to reveal their passwords. I'm a journalist, I'm good at this stuff. Damn it, you're a copper, you should be good at it too. Don't you know anybody who could hack into her computer? There must be some bad lad that you know?'

'Jesus Emmy, I want to get my hands on the cash, but I'm not doing that. I'd go to prison and there's a lot of hard bastards in there who could make my life a misery.'

'You need to lean on Cait and see what her plans are. If it comes to it, you should tell her that if she gives you a cut of it, you'll push off and leave her to her new fortune. That's if she wants rid of you. Offer to make it easy for her. A clean break for, what, 100k? That should do it. We'll be set up with that amount of cash – once Porter pushes off, that is.'

'Do you think he suspects what's going on?'

'Porter? The man's barely alive, I don't think he notices anything.'

'Why on earth did you two get together?'

'Why does anyone get together? Why did you and Cait become a couple?'

'I'm serious. Me and Cait got along fine for a while. It's only since we hooked up that I've seen her faults. We were never marriage and kids material, although I think she once thought we might be. How about you?'

'What? Kids? I'm not really interested. Porter is, but he's ten years older than me. I've got my career on the paper, it's exciting, I like to be in the thick of things. Porter's just ... dull. When we met, I thought he was distinguished and intelligent. I was stupid enough to marry him before I realised he was just a boring little man.'

Emmy's phone vibrated.

'That's the office. There's a full staff meeting at ten – are we going out for breakfast?'

Terry leaned over to pick up his phone. His back was as densely populated with hair as his chest. When the body hair was being handed out, Terry got three times the regular allocation. Emmy liked that, a man who looked like a man. It was good to spend the night with a simple guy like Terry.

He texted Caitlen to put her off the scent.

We got them good and proper. Video evidence of them handing over the drugs. Well worth an all-nighter. See you later, T.

He thought about adding a kiss before sending the text. He decided to add two, he wanted her to feel like he was going to be difficult to get rid of. What a dance it was, both of them wanting the relationship to end but neither of them confronting the issue until it was the right time and place for them. Emmy and Porter were the same. Terry was not a deep-thinking man, but he did sometimes wonder how many relationships were based on complete bullshit. They were all going through the motions until the point at which somebody finally decided to call time on it. In the meantime, they supported the lie.

'Breakfast would be good. There are a couple of places along this road, I think. I can't face the breakfast here, it's continental rubbish. I might just as well eat the Bible in that drawer for all the taste those croissants have.'

Emmy got out of bed. She was still naked, they both were. Terry imagined a life with this woman by his side. Just looking at her walking across the room made him hot. She was his kind of woman: straightforward, funny and really dirty in bed. It was a dream come true. He'd never been with a woman like that before. As a journalist she knew his world. That's how they'd met, both working a job, only he was trying to find out who'd left the body and she was trying to report on it. They'd hit it off immediately.

Terry resisted the temptation to encourage Emmy back into bed. She'd need to shower – after what they'd been up to, she wouldn't want to go into the office without cleaning up first. Besides, in Benidorm it would be hard – probably impossible – to get any time alone together. They needed to chat and make a plan. Benidorm was going to be their moment. He was going to end it after the visit to Spain, but he was determined not to leave empty-handed.

By the time Emmy had showered, dressed and put on her make-up, Terry was also cleaned up and ready to go. They checked out of the hotel and walked up the street, looking in the windows of the cafés that were open and deciding what they wanted to eat for breakfast.

'What will we do in Spain, Ems? Do you think we'll be able to sneak off from the others?'

'We should find something to do that the others won't be interested in. Walking or something like that.'

Terry stopped outside a burger bar to examine the menu.

'This looks good. They do bacon rolls and you can always get a decent coffee in these places.'

'Looks great,' Emmy replied, thinking how Porter would have dragged her into some hippy place that served avocado on toast or eggs Benedict, some crap like that. She was a journalist, and as a journalist she lived on bacon butties and coffee. Just like coppers.

They pushed through the double doors and joined the back of the short queue. Terry held Emmy's hand, moving close into her while they waited and made final decisions on what they were eating. Soon they'd be together. Soon. If they could only walk away with some of Caitlen's cash in the bank, it would be perfect.

'How may I help you this morning? We have a free extra topping with every long macchiato that you order today.'

Terry didn't even know what one of those was, it sounded like an opera to him.

The penny was slow to drop for Terry, but Emmy had picked it up straightaway. The red cap and hair tied back in a ponytail together with the uniform made her look like all the other employees. It was the voice that did it and made her look twice.

'Well, fancy that! What on earth are you doing here, Naomi?'

'I might ask you two the same thing,' Naomi said, as Terry drew his hand away from Emmy's, horrified to see who was serving them.

TEN

Benidorm: June

WHAT A PRAT!' Terry said, openly sneering at Wes. This new arrival was definitely not his kind of man. Caitlen, Naomi and Harriet were hovering around him, enthralled by his wonderful guitar playing and incredible singing voice.

'Singing James Blunt, too. I think I just died and went to hell.'

Terry tried a joke as soon as he realised which song Wes was singing.

'Yeah, you're beautiful too, mate, but if I see your face in a crowded place I'll know exactly what to do.'

His lyric-based satire fell on deaf ears.

'I really like James Blunt,' Rhett protested, as if the singer were in the room with them and had taken offence at Terry's comments. 'He's sold a shedload of albums. For some reason lots of blokes seem to have a real problem with him, but he was in the army before he was a pop star – he can't be a prat because they'd have sorted him out there if he was.'

'Actually, I like him too,' Kasey agreed.

'Well, you would, wouldn't you?' Terry said. He back-pedalled quickly. 'What I mean is that guys who are gay are more sensitive, aren't they? I mean you dress better than us straight guys and you have better taste in music. And you can dance ...'

Rhett rescued him.

'Whatever you think of James Blunt, you can't deny that Wes is amazing.'

Terry couldn't deny that Wes was amazing. It was cramping his style already.

Matt and Becky walked through the open apartment door. They'd been drawn by the sound of the music making its way along the hallway.

'What is that lovely sound? I thought you'd put a CD on,' Becky said.

'It's Wes, he's amazing!' Caitlen replied quietly, as Wes brought the song to an end and acknowledged the round of applause.

'Yeah, him and James, they're a right couple of Blunts!' Terry muttered in earshot of the men. Still there were no bites.

'Actually, I'm partial to a bit of James Blunt,' Matt said. 'I loved his first album, couldn't stop playing it when it came out.'

'Maybe we should adopt "You're Beautiful" as our tune?' Becky suggested.

It was Matt's turn to mutter something inaudible. He'd just spent the afternoon in bed with Becky, supposedly sleeping off that day's journey. He looked like a man who was getting deeper and deeper into a trap.

Wes started to play a new tune.

'See if you recognise this one,' he announced. He was performing already, he had a rapt audience and he hadn't even ventured away from the sofa in Caitlen's apartment yet.

They recognised the tune immediately.

'Oh, I love a bit of Oasis, what a great choice,' said Harriet. 'It's like having your own private jukebox. This is amazing, Wes!'

'Hi, mind if I come in?'

It was Gina, drawn in by the excitement in the apartment opposite hers. There was a moment of disappointment as the men turned around to find that she was now fully clothed. But she was looking stunning in a figure-hugging short dress, her long legs smooth and muscular, her figure toned and athletic.

'Hi Gina!' Caitlen said, a little over-enthusiastically.

She'd immediately warmed to this woman but didn't want to come over as her needy fat friend. In fact, Caitlen was in excellent shape for someone who was almost ten years Gina's senior, but the sight of the younger woman dressed for a night out, fresh-faced and exuberant, made her only too aware that time was slipping away.

'Mind if I listen?' Gina said. 'It sounds fantastic!'

'Come in, come in!' Caitlen encouraged her. 'We're heading out for some food and drink in a while. We've all recovered from the flight now and we're ready to take a look around. You're welcome to join us ... if you're not doing anything else.'

'I'd love to,' Gina replied. 'If you don't mind me tagging along?'

'Of course not, the more the merrier!' said Rhett.

'Excellent, thank you. I was heading out on my own this evening, it'll be lovely to have some company.'

Caitlen envied her independence. She'd sung along with the Spice Girls in her younger days, but whatever had become of her own girl power? There was a time, probably around Gina's age, when she would have despised herself for staying with Terry a moment longer. But age had taught her that life is more complicated than that. Sometimes, through no fault of your own, you get stuck with a Terry.

Emmy and Porter arrived.

'Jeez, are you vaping?' Terry asked, before he'd even said hello.

'Yes, I'm trying to give up the ciggies,' Porter replied.

He looked like he was sucking on a child's toy. The earnest way in which he used the device made it look like he was dependent on it for his life.

'What a prat!' Emmy whispered to Terry, her words concealed by Wes's passionate portrayal of 'Don't Look Back In Anger'.

'Who, Wes or Porter?' Terry replied.

'Both! Oh, and James bloody Blunt too. I heard that racket from our apartment. How long do we have to put up with this caterwauling?'

Terry stood up, interrupting the song's finale.

'John Smiths anybody?'

There were no replies, so he headed over to the fridge and took out two cans.

'Here,' he said, handing one to Emmy.

There was a round of applause as Wes's enchanted audience waited for the final guitar note to fade into nothingness.

'That's amazing, Wes!'

'Incredible. I love it!'

'Wow, thanks guys. Let's hope they like it as much in town. I could do with a gig in one of the bars, I'm running a bit low on funds.'

'You should call in at Erin's Bar,' said Gina. 'You do covers, right? Anybody in particular?'

'Yeah, well, I do lots of stuff, but James Blunt, Ed Sheeran ... I do that guy-with-guitar stuff. What do they want at Erin's Bar?'

'They do cover bands. They'd love you, I'm sure of it. It's been on the telly, you might even know it. They film some of the scenes from that TV series in there, the one that's set in Benidorm.'

'Oh, I've seen that!' Becky said. 'I didn't even realise it was a real bar.' It turned out that most of them had seen the TV programme. Within three minutes, Erin's Bar had become the most sought-after location in the town.

Terry was pleased that the focus had changed and that it finally looked like they were on their way.

'I didn't know you drank John Smiths,' Caitlen said, observing the can in Emmy's hand.

'Oh, yes, it's a recent thing,' Emmy blustered. 'A girl can have too much Prosecco. And it rots your teeth if you drink too much of it, you know.'

It was a long answer for an off-the-cuff observation. If she hadn't been quite so detailed in her reply, Caitlen might not have clocked it. She put it to the back of her mind and diverted her attention to encouraging everybody out into the hallway.

'What are we going for, Indian or Chinese?' Rhett asked, taking the lead.

By the time they'd all made their way down in the lifts, they'd decided they were eating Italian. Pizza to be precise. They'd eat together on the first night, but be flexible in the days ahead to accommodate everybody's food tastes.

Terry was still carrying his can of beer when they walked out into the street. It was early evening, still light and sunny and the street was alive with holiday-makers. It was a sea of cheap sunglasses, baseball caps, sandals, cargo shorts and garish T-shirts. Terry became immediately invisible, the others less so.

Gina guided them to an Italian restaurant and they enjoyed an early evening meal fuelled by familiar wines and beers which had been stocked to please a predominantly British clientele. The serving staff spoke impressive English and if it hadn't been for the stunning blue sky outside and the invigorating warmth of the sun, they could just have easily been in Blackpool. Only there, as Terry observed, the sea would have looked like a muddy puddle and the sky would have been as grey as Porter's hair.

In response, Porter took a crafty suck on his vaper, checking that he hadn't been spotted by the staff. He'd got away with it.

'After all, it's not really smoking, is it?' he said to Naomi, who was sitting next to him at the table.

'Well, actually, Porter it is really, isn't it?'

He looked stunned by that.

'I see people all the time in the ... when I'm out. I see people in restaurants ignoring the No Smoking signs and when you challenge them about it, they say it's not smoking. Well it is. Only we don't know yet how much rubbish they put in those things and what harm it can do to you.'

Porter avoided a debate on the issue. Instead, he placed the device in his back pocket and looked chastened. Terry and Emmy exchanged a smirk. Both had given up smoking some years previously, in spite of it being so prevalent in their professions. They could now gloat at those still strug-gling to quit. Besides, any time Porter got called out for being an idiot, it was something to be celebrated. He and Caitlen were their only obstacles to being together, out in the open. And soon both of them would be out of the way.

ELEVEN

Benidorm: June

'DAMN, that sounds good. Much better than that nonsense Wes was playing.'

Terry had already drunk a little more than he should have and his mouth was starting to run away with the excitement of it all. They'd gone along the seafront to walk off their pizza and had been drawn to a bar from which the sound of heavy rock tunes was emanating.

Wes ignored the comment, he was used to loud mouths in the audience.

It might sound better if you stop trying to strangle it, mate!

Do you know any decent songs?

Will somebody please put that cat out of its misery!

Men like Terry were par for the course in his line of work. It was the women it brought into his orbit who made it all worthwhile. There's something about a man who can make music. It worked like a charm for Wes. He'd travel the bars, playing covers of hit tunes, making a bit of money and getting laid along the way. He was a young bloke with no ties, what else would he do? Besides, he'd had to leave Thailand in a rush. He'd overstayed his welcome there.

For Wes, Benidorm had everything he needed: British holiday-makers, hundreds of bars which catered to their every need, and gullible women like Caitlen who'd take him at face value without a second thought about who he might be. She'd been standing right next to him in the passport queue and if she'd taken the trouble to glance at his passport, she'd have seen that the first thing he'd told her was a lie. His name was not Wesley Nolasco. He'd chosen that name on a whim. Now that he'd all but seduced them with his music, he had them hook, line and sinker. He was already a part of the group – it was as if he'd always been around.

'You're incredibly talented,' Gina said, moving up closer to him as Rhett and Terry played air guitar behind them on the pavement.

'Thank you, I appreciate it!' he said, giving his best charming smile. 'Thanks for the tip-off about Erin's Bar, too. That sounds like just my kind of place. Once the heavy metal festival ends, I hope we can go there so I can check it out.'

'It's fun, they have all sorts of acts on. I don't know if they have any open slots, but it'll be a good start if nothing else.'

'How long have you been out here?' Wes asked.

'I'm a traveller,' Gina said. 'I don't live anywhere in particular, I don't have a bloke or a woman in tow, so I please myself.'

'What's your preferred type of music? I take it a lady like you isn't into this stuff?'

AC/DC's 'Whole Lotta Rosie' was now blaring out of the speakers. Terry and Rhett were back to back on a beach-front bench playing air guitar. Anybody passing might have mistaken them for Angus and Malcolm Young. On a second look, they'd have realised it was just a couple of British idiots.

'Oh, I love a bit of rock and roll at times. I like this stuff. But when I'm working I like it quieter. David Gray, Dido, Coldplay. That sort of thing. Do you play David Gray?'

'Yeah, I reckon I could still manage "Babylon", although it's a while since I've played it. I'll do it tonight if they let me on stage.'

'Wow, really? Thank you, what a treat.'

The others had begun to gather away from the bar and were looking out over towards the sea. Harriet was there, not really taking part in the conversation. The loners were always the easiest for Wes. Nobody to get in the way and make life difficult.

'We should join the others,' he said to Gina. 'I think those two will have burned themselves out soon.'

As 'Whole Lotta Rosie' ended and Terry and Rhett came to the realisation that they were not in fact on stage at Wembley, the consensus was that it was time to move on. Terry was dripping with sweat. Rhett, the fitter of the two, regained his composure swiftly.

'Okay, we need to regroup,' Caitlen said.

She was not the leader, but as she was bankrolling the entire holiday, she felt duty-bound to keep things on track. So far it had felt like herding cats.

'I propose a gentle walk along the beach before Terry dies from a heart attack, then we head for Erin's Bar. Everybody okay with that?'

'It's quite a walk along the beach,' Gina said. 'If you follow me, I'll lead the way.'

They split off into their groups. Terry, Emmy and Rhett moved off towards the sea away from the walkway. Matt tried to resist Becky pulling away as a couple. He made a vain attempt to include Naomi in the conversation, but Becky was having none of it. She took Matt's hand and fell back from the main group.

'I'm going to run ahead,' Wes said.

He'd brought his guitar with him, ready to put on a show at the drop of a hat if he got a bite in one of the bars.

He put his hand up as a parting gesture, smiled at Gina and moved into the crowd of holiday-makers enjoying the last of the day's sunshine.

Kasey and Harriet, who might have been a couple had their gender preferences been different, walked on with Naomi and Porter. The debate about vaping had flared up again, and as a former smoker himself Kasey was now siding with Porter and his right to choose. It was more friendly now, there was a lot more laughter, Naomi realised she'd been too quick off the mark in condemning her friend. She'd almost bitten his head off. She'd was always quick to a temper.

Caitlen was ecstatic to be left alone with Gina. She hung back a little, making sure that they stayed ahead of Matt and Becky but didn't catch up with the vaping debating society. She didn't care about the argument and couldn't care less what Porter did. He never smoked in their house, that was all she cared about.

'It's lovely, isn't it?' said Gina. 'People call this place Blackpool with sun but it's much better than that. I love it here. You've got the buses and the tram, you're ten minutes from the most incredible countryside. And the weather's amazing.'

'You know, I'm really quite envious of you, Gina. How do you do it, living on your own, with no job or house to worry about? I'd love to do what you do.'

'Aren't you and Terry married – do you have kids?'

With one short sentence, Gina had got to the heart of it.

'No, we don't have kids and we're not married.'

Gina said nothing.

'Truth be told, we're chalk and cheese. As you can probably tell from his heavy rock performance back there.'

Gina laughed.

'It was quite something, wasn't it? How do you know Wes? He's not one of your group, is he?'

'No, I picked him up at the airport. Not like that, of course. I don't really know how we picked him up actually. He just tagged along. But what a performer!'

'I don't want to piss on your parade, but just be wary of Wes. I meet a lot of guys like him on the road. They're chancers. Wherever I lay my hat and all that. He's tried his luck with me already. If he plays a David Gray song on stage during this holiday, believe me, he's a freeloader. I just don't want you to be taken advantage of.'

Caitlen changed the subject, she hadn't even thought to question Wes's motives.

'This beach is fantastic.'

Naomi's group had stopped walking and were waiting for Gina to catch up so they could check how far they had to walk.

'It's a little way to go yet. You're not going flaky on me, are you? If you think this is a long way, you should try the walk up to the Benidorm Cross up there!'

Gina pointed ahead of her into the distance. On a hill,

overlooking the resort and behind the high-rise buildings was a large cross.

'Can you walk up there?' Naomi asked. 'It looks really high up.'

'It's quite a hike if you're not used to walking long distances, but it's not that difficult. Just pace yourself and bring some water to cool yourself down, you don't need to be an athlete to get up there.'

Terry, Rhett and Emmy joined the group, half hearing the conversation.

'Are you talking about walking all the way up to that cross?' Rhett asked.

'We are,' Naomi answered. 'If you think you could manage it after your heavy metal escapades.'

'Walk all the way up there?' Emmy said, her eyes searching for the cross. 'Over my dead body!'

TWELVE

Matt and Becky: April

'WELL, I think she was a right cow upstaging us like that. It's our engagement – news doesn't come any bigger than that!'

Becky had been fractious since they'd returned from Caitlen's dinner party. Matt was preoccupied with his earlier encounter with Harriet in the kitchen. They'd almost been caught, but it felt delicious – dangerous, daring and exhilarating. And now he was back in his prison cell, like a dog on a lead, itching to run off into the distance but constrained by his owner.

How had he got himself into this state? It was a classic rebound scenario, only he'd been stupid enough to take refuge with Becky. Now, Becky was hot, she was a great looking woman and any man would be proud to be seen out with her. But she was unstable. It's the only way Matt could describe it. He knew that mental illness could be a sensitive issue, he had every sympathy with anybody experiencing it. But Becky was dangerous. He didn't know how it would be described in medical terms. He'd looked it up online. It was psychosis, as far as he could tell, doing his amateur doctor research. She appeared to be delusional, perhaps even bipolar at times. She was up and down a lot, but he only got a real sense of that when he was spending every day with her. And now he'd signed up for that, he felt completely trapped.

He'd always fancied Becky physically and she'd made it very clear from the first day that they'd met – at another one of Caitlen's get-togethers, ironically enough – that she wanted him. It had been a cause of tension between him and Harriet at the time.

'She wants to jump your bones, that's really bloody rude of her to make it so obvious while I'm around.'

'She's only messing around and you know I'm not interested. She's attractive, sure, but she's not marriage material. She can be pretty tempestuous at times.'

That would make Harriet prickly, the talk of marriage and the implied suggestion of babies. She wasn't ready for that yet, and any mention of it pressed the wrong buttons for her. It was a discussion just like that which had caused Matt to flee to Becky in the first place.

'Do you think she'll share the money out? I mean, maybe chip in and help with the wedding. She could pay for the honeymoon as a present.'

Becky broke Matt's train of thought. The truth was, since being with her he'd recognised a little bit of himself in her. That neediness. He'd pressured Harriet too much. He loved Harriet and wanted to marry her. He desired nothing more than to think about a life of marital bliss and babies.

But he'd come on too strong, Harriet needed more time. And in his impetuousness, he'd blown the best relationship he'd ever had. And exchanged it for this one with Becky.

'You can't think like that, Becky,' he replied. 'It's Cait's money and we should be grateful that she's treating us to the trip to Spain. I'd say that's quite enough, wouldn't you?'

'No,' Becky replied, taut and suddenly very defensive. 'We've been friends with her and Naomi for a couple of years now, it's how you and I met. Friends look after friends. They don't get rich and leave them behind. Especially when they're getting married.'

Becky had a weird logic which Matt couldn't get his head around. He made the foolish error of trying to set her right.

'Cait doesn't owe us anything, Becky. Besides, the money she has is wonderful, but she's hardly rich. It's more like a cash windfall. She'll be able to buy a nice house, put some in the bank, maybe even get herself a holiday home. But it's not enough to set her up for life.'

'Why do you always support other people, Matt? You never support me. You're going to be my husband soon. We're a unit. We should be on the same page about these things.'

Matt saw the wild look in her eyes. It was time for him to back off. If he wound her up any more, what followed might get ugly. He wondered if he dared to end it there and then. If he walked out – right at that moment – would she just get over it? Would all the threats she'd made last time prove to be empty? He shuddered when he thought back to it. He'd only mentioned how nice Harriet had been looking at a meal they'd been to as a smaller group. Becky had flown off the handle.

'I don't want you to see that slut ever again. She's not good for you, she poisons your mind against me. She still wants you, even though she broke it off with you. Leave her alone!'

'But we have to see her still, she's part of our group. We can't not talk to her. You at least have to be polite to her.'

'She's a whore and I want you to stay away from her. If you ever got together again I don't know what I'd do. I'd kill myself, that's what I'd do. If I lost you to her, you'd find me dead, right here in this house!'

Becky grabbed a kitchen knife with a serrated edge. She held it against her wrist and pressed down on the skin.

Only the week before, Matt had cut his finger on that knife. It was sharp and deadly, it had hurt.

'Or maybe I'll slit my throat. That will show you how much I love you. Then you'll regret ever being with that slag. I'd kill her too, that would teach her to try and steal you away from me.'

Matt didn't know what to do. The knife was being waved around precariously, one slip and she'd cut herself.

'Becky darling, calm down. It's over with me and Harriet. You said it yourself, she threw me out, she ended it. And now I'm with you. And we're ... we're going to be married soon.'

The words stuck in his throat as he said them.

Matt watched as Becky relaxed her grip on the knife.

'I'm telling you, Matt, if you ever go back to that woman again, you'll find me here hanging from a rope tied to the loft rafters. I've worked it all out, I don't care. If it comes to it, I'll either use the knife or hang myself on the landing. And you'll be the one who's responsible. You and Harriet.'

Becky and Harriet used to be friends. They would talk and laugh together, though when Matt looked back he realised that Becky had probably only tolerated Harriet to get to him. Perhaps she'd planned it that way all along, she was manipulative enough.

Matt tried to change the subject. He wanted Becky to put the knife away.

'I thought you looked amazing tonight. I love that dress, it really suits you.'

The change in Becky was immediate. She placed the knife on the kitchen worktop.

'Naomi complimented me on it too. She said it made my figure look stunning.'

'I agree. And your hair looks great. It shows off your beautiful neck.'

Becky walked away from the knife, put her arms around him and pulled him in towards her.

'I like it best when it's just me and you,' she said, kissing his neck. 'We're like little love birds and this house is our nest.'

Matt was relieved that the situation hadn't escalated. He pulled Becky in towards him, not wanting to give her any inkling that his mind was elsewhere. It was Harriet he was imagining, pressed in close to him, her smell intoxicating, her body like an enchanting potion.

'You know, Caitlen was really careless this evening.'

'Why?' Matt replied, wondering where this was heading.

'Do you remember when we'd all moved into the lounge and she was giving everybody their passwords?'

'Yes, I can't stop repeating mine in my head. I'm terrified of forgetting it.'

'Remember when her mobile phone went off and she took the call? You were looking at the pictures on the wall.'

Matt nodded. They were still close together, he could look directly into Becky's eyes. She was calm again now.

'I took a photo of the full list. She just left it there on the table. I couldn't resist it. She said that she shredded it after she'd spoken to all of us, but I have a photo of it. It's on my phone.'

'Damn, Becky, you shouldn't have done that!'

She moved away from him. He'd felt her tense up the moment he'd dared to venture that he might have a different opinion.

'Why not?' she asked. 'If Caitlen was stupid enough to leave it there in the open, that's her lookout.'

'But she trusts us, Becky. We're her friends. She wanted us to help her keep that information secure. And now you've broken that trust. You should delete the image.'

'Sod that!' Becky laughed. 'If she doesn't help us out with the wedding of her own accord, I'll tell her that I've got her precious bloody passwords. I'll be fair, I'll give her a chance to offer first. But if she leaves us high and dry ... well, screw her. I'll either force her into giving us some or I'll figure out how to take it for myself.'

'Hell, Becky, you can't do that! If the full password fell into the wrong hands, she could lose all her money. You don't want that, do you?'

Becky had moved away from him now and was edging back towards the kitchen knife. Matt could feel himself sweating at the temples. Is this what domestic abuse is like? he wondered. Is this how it begins, with manipulation and threats?

'If she's as good a friend as she claims to be, she'll help us out with the wedding without being prompted. We announced our engagement on the same night as she broke her news. She should be pleased to celebrate her good fortune with us. And if she's not ... well, she'll regret it.'

Matt looked towards Becky. In that moment he saw her for what she truly was. And it frightened him. He now had no idea what this woman was capable of or what else she might have been plotting in her disturbed mind.

THIRTEEN

Benidorm: June

AS THEY WALKED into Erin's Bar, things were in full flow.

'I've fallen in love with Benidorm!' Terry declared. 'Not only is it not throwing it down with rain all the time, they serve John Smiths beer everywhere.'

'What's the big deal with John Smiths?' Porter asked.

'In the UK you can't get a decent pint any more. Everything is either some speciality beer brewed by guys with beards long enough to sleep in or they're flavoured with Himalayan herbs extracted from the arses of mountain goats. I just want a regular pint of beer, not some weird concoction dreamed up by a youngster who's barely out of school.'

'Terry struggles with the modern world, don't you, mate?' Rhett laughed, placing his hand affectionately on Terry's shoulder. 'We went out for a coffee once and he insisted on getting a Nescafé. It was hilarious. They kept offering him espressos, lattes, cappuccinos ... the lot. And he was standing there saying I just want a Nescafé please! The sad thing is, the kids who were serving him didn't even know what he was talking about.'

There was general laughter at Terry's expense and the first round was bought by Caitlen who was anxious that none of them should be spending their own cash.

'I wonder how Wes got on?' Naomi asked. 'I can't see him anywhere, can you?'

'This woman is very good. She looks just like Lady Gaga,' Harriet said, referring to the tribute act who was on stage performing covers of famous songs. The venue was packed. Caitlen was happy about the genial atmosphere. This was a good place to be.

'I can recognise it from the telly,' Terry said. 'Look, that's the bar with the fish tank. They're always filming stuff over there.'

Porter had managed to find a spare table and Rhett, Becky and Matt had gone over to help him find some extra chairs to give everybody a seat. Harriet and Gina were talking at the bar. Naomi seemed to be hovering while Caitlen was waiting for her own drink to be served and to settle up the bill.

'You alright, sis?' she asked. 'I was hoping to have a quick word with you. It's a bit loud in here. Can we step outside for five minutes?'

'Sure. Is everything alright?'

'Yes, of course. I just felt that we should chat – away from Terry and Rhett, they always turn everything into a joke.'

'At least Terry does!' Caitlen smiled.

They carried their drinks outside and grabbed a small table which had just been vacated by a smoker.

'What is it?'

Naomi looked uncomfortable and Caitlen sensed that something awkward was coming. She'd half expected it after their talk in the apartment. Naomi seemed to have something on her mind.

'How are you planning to spend the money?' she blurted out. 'I mean ... are you planning to sha ... will you be investing any of it?'

'I don't know yet,' Caitlen replied.

She seemed to be speaking a lot about money recently. She hadn't even got her hands on most of it yet, and already she could feel the vultures circling. Most of them hadn't said anything, but she could tell it was preying on their minds, like an itch that they just couldn't scratch.

'Do you think ... will you be sharing any of it out?'

'What do you mean?' Caitlen replied tersely.

She hadn't even settled on her own plans yet and already everybody wanted to spend her cash for her. Naomi took a large sip of her G&T and finally said what she wanted to say.

'Will any of it be coming my way? Me and Rhett, will we be getting any of it?'

Her face reddened. She'd clearly been working her way up to this.

'Does Rhett know we're having this conversation? Did he put you up to it?'

'No ... yes ... no ... not really. I just wondered, only ...'

'Only what?'

'I just wondered, that's all. It's a lot of money and I thought that you might be sharing some of it out.'

'What, more than I have done already you mean? I'm paying for this holiday, Naomi. What else did you have in mind?'

'I just thought--'

'Look, I can't even think that far ahead. I told you where I'm up to with Terry. Every crass thing he's done on this holiday so far makes me cringe. I'm going to finish it when we get home. I can't do it here, it would be horrible for the rest of you. But I haven't got my hands on the money yet. It's not even in my bank account – how can I even think about what I'm spending it on before I see how much I've got? Besides, I was going to treat you again once you'd all handed back the passwords that I'd given you. As a thank you.'

Naomi looked chastened. That very morning they'd missed another mortgage payment. She'd switched on her mobile phone as she got off the plane and it was the first message waiting for her when the backlog of messages started coming in.

'I was going to give you all a weekend break as a thank you. With a five hundred pound budget. Don't tell the others yet, will you? I don't want to mention it before I tell Terry. I don't want him making plans for the future.'

At any other time, the holiday in Benidorm and a weekend away with Rhett would have been more than enough for Naomi. It was only because of their financial difficulties that matters were so pressing. And then she saw it, the link, the connection that would give her the leverage that she needed. She was keeping Terry and Emmy's dirty little secret. They'd agreed to stay quiet after they discovered her working in the burger bar and she'd said that she would reciprocate. She was also keeping Caitlen's secret: that she was going to leave Terry, empty-handed too. They were allies in this, between them they had several passwords. Without the passwords, Caitlen had none of her precious money.

'It's okay, Cait. I shouldn't have said anything,' she said, picking up her drink. 'You've been more than generous, thank you. I'm sorry.'

Naomi stood up, touched her sister on the shoulder, then went back into the bar. She was so caught up in her own thoughts that she brushed straight past Porter who was skulking in the corner, puffing on his vaper. At first he went to speak to her, but she hadn't spotted him there. He'd caught the gist of the conversation from afar. He turned away so that he was looking down the street.

Caitlen decided to nurse her drink a little longer.

'Hello you, I wondered where you'd got to!'

It was Gina. She pulled Caitlen away from her thoughts.

'Hi Gina, I'm pleased it's you. They're wearing me out that lot in there. We're supposed to be friends, but you can't really be best friends with everybody, can you?'

'What do you mean?' Gina said, pulling up a chair.

'Well, we call ourselves a group of friends, but no group of friends can like each member equally, can they? I mean, Becky plays polite with Harriet, but the two of them hate each other. Porter comes as part of the package with Emmy, but he's a bit of a prat, if truth be told. Matt still fancies Harriet and looks like he can't wait to push Becky over a cliff edge. And Becky ... well, I'm not certain she likes anybody at all, herself included. Kasey seems to be the only universally liked person in the group. Yet we call ourselves a group of friends.'

'Where did all this come from?' Gina asked, genuinely concerned. The two women had established an immediate rapport.

'Oh, I don't know. Have you heard of bitcoin? It's a

cryptocurrency, you've probably seen it mentioned in the papers.'

'Yes, I own some. How do you think I manage to swan around like I do? Sure, I work because you can't play all the time, but I bought some myself. It's been very good to me.'

'Where do you keep yours?' Caitlen asked, immediately interested that her new friend knew what she was talking about.

'You have to be careful with it, it's very easy to steal. It's best not to tell people where you keep it. It's a precarious business – if you leave it on your laptop, you can be hacked and have it all stolen.'

'I found that out for myself. That's why we're here in Benidorm. All my friends have part of my password, but no single person has the entire thing. I was terrified of leaving it on my phone or a computer. I did some research and decided to store it on a special gadget – like a USB drive but more secure. That's the best way to do it, as far as I can tell.'

'Your instincts are right, Caitlen, and you've done your research well, but I hope you've put your storage device in a safe place. If that gets stolen you're in big trouble.'

Gina could see from the look on Caitlen's face that she hadn't done that.

'Don't tell me ... Where did you leave it? Not under the mattress, please, not under the mattress.'

'No, not as bad as that. I was scared of losing it. I thought about leaving it at home, but I panicked at the last minute – I wanted to keep it in my sight.'

'Where is it?' Gina asked. 'Of course, you don't have to tell me if you don't want to, but please put it somewhere really secure.'

'Seriously? That seems a bit over the top.'

'Do you have a decent amount of money on yours?'

'Enough to make a difference, yes.'

Caitlen adjusted her bra strap, it felt tight all of a sudden.

'You haven't, have you?'

Caitlen's face reddened. She nodded.

'It's in your bra?'

'Wrapped in tissue and taped to my D-cup, yes. It's the only place I could think of where it would be absolutely safe. Well, the only hygienic place!'

'Promise me you'll come into town with me tomorrow morning and we'll place it in a private mailbox. I'll talk you through it, and you need to do the same thing when you get back to the UK. Promise?'

'Yes, I promise,' Caitlen replied sheepishly. 'It's just that seemed the safest way to protect it. And who else do you trust if you can't trust your friends?'

FOURTEEN

Benidorm: June

GINA SPOTTED IT FIRST. They were topping up their drinks at the bar and she'd offered to pay for the round.

'Is that chap who's just sat down next to Becky called Porter?'

'Yes, why?' Caitlen asked.

'Someone needs to shout at him to let him know his arse is on fire, that's why.'

'Oh Jesus, his vaper is smoking in his back pocket.'

Caitlen rushed over to the table, but Porter had already figured out what was going on. He was screaming so loud it could be heard over the music. There was a new cover band on playing Queen's 'Don't Stop Me Now'. Even as she helped Porter, Caitlen thought how good they sounded.

Everybody was standing up now, helping Porter. Becky, Matt, Rhett, Kasey and Naomi all fussed around him. It caused such a commotion that the band leader stopped halfway through the song.

'Are you all right, mate?'

All eyes in the Tavern turned towards Porter. He was pulling off his trousers in a panic. As his legs became visible, the extent of his wounds could be seen. There was a collective gasp from the other drinkers as they saw the damage that had been done to Porter's leg.

'Oi, the song's called 'Don't Stop Me Now', so why have you stopped playing?'

Caitlen recognised the voice immediately. It was Terry. Worse than that, it was drunk, loud, noisy and offensive Terry.

'What's he doing over there?' Caitlen asked, distracted for a moment.

'Dancing with Emmy,' Kasey replied, 'They've been at it ever since they started playing "Crazy Little Thing Called Love".'

'I didn't think those two had that much in common,' she said, turning back to Porter. His leg was a mess, burned and bloody.

'Is he alright?' the lead singer asked over the microphone. 'Would one of the bar staff call for an ambulance?'

Two members of the bar staff escorted Porter over to a chair tucked behind the counter. The band started to play a new song and before long the rest of the drinkers at Erin's Bar had got back to their beers and singalong.

'Had somebody better go over and tell Emmy what's happened? She and Terry seem oblivious to what's going on.'

It was Kasey who suggested it.

Terry was back to the air guitar with Emmy dancing around him as his fingers moved frantically over an imaginary fretboard.

'I'll go,' Caitlen said. 'Somebody just stay with Porter please until the ambulance comes.'

Caitlen walked over to Terry and Emmy. They were tucked away from the main area, dancing at the side of the room with a few other drunkards.

'You're drunk, Terry!' Caitlen said, disapprovingly.

'And you've got a face like a pit bull chewing a toffee!' he responded, not bothering to interrupt his guitar solo.

'Porter's had an accident, Emmy. He needs to go to the hospital. You should go with him.'

'Porter's always having accidents,' she said in a slurred voice. 'That fool is a walking accident.'

'Shut up moaning and give us your money. I'm ready for another drink,' said Terry.

Caitlen ignored him. This was no time for a debate.

'He's pretty badly burned, Ems. His e-cigarette exploded in his back pocket. It's done some serious damage.'

The song ended and the band started to play 'Bohemian Rhapsody'. The bar erupted into cheers. Terry and Emmy readied themselves for an operatic duet. Caitlen gave up on them, they were too far gone. They wouldn't thank her for sending a drunk Emmy in the ambulance with Porter.

'She's the worse for wear, I suggest that somebody else goes with Porter. Who's game? I'm paying the bills, remember, so I'd better hang around here.'

There was a general lack of enthusiasm. Porter cried out as one of the bar staff attempted to place a cotton-wool pad over his wounds. He was keen to remind them all that he was still there.

The ambulance team entered the bar.

'Damn, that was fast!' Rhett laughed. 'Nothing like the UK. You'd have been dead before they turned up.'

Nobody was in the mood for it. They were relieved that

help had arrived. The paramedics seemed surprised to be dealing with a sober Brit for once. It was a genuine casualty. They knew exactly what to do with Porter and immediately got on with cleaning up the wound.

'So who's going with him?' Caitlen asked again.

Rhett, Naomi, Harriet, Becky, Matt and Kasey looked at each other. Gina was absolved by virtue of her being a tag-along. She'd barely had a chance to get to know Porter.

Kasey broke first of all.

'I'll go,' he said. 'I was rather hoping to check out one of the gay bars in town tonight. Looks like that will have to wait now.'

The others were relieved. They hung around long enough to wave Porter and Kasey off in the ambulance, then headed back into the bar, greeted by the fading notes of 'We Are The Champions'.

'Thank you, you've been amazing!' the lead singer said, his amplified voice filling the space. 'We play here every night but Saturday, so we'll see you again soon. Coming up next, a change to the advertised programme. It's a new singer called Wes Nolasco and he's going to be playing some wonderful songs for you. He'll be up in five minutes … goodnight!'

There was a huge cheer. Terry and Emmy worked their way back to the bar, deprived of their music now and desperate to refuel themselves via Caitlen's endless bar tab.

'I was going to suggest moving on,' Caitlen said, 'but we'd better hang around long enough to show Wes some support. What do you say?'

'Will he be playing more of that Ed Sheeran rubbish?' Terry asked. His arm was now around Emmy's waist. She removed it, giving him a stern look.

'If you mean acoustic songs, then yes, I think he will be,' Naomi replied.

'Mind if we move on then?' Rhett asked. 'There's a rockier bar along this street. Can we meet up with you there? Are you coming, Tez?'

'Of course I'm coming,' Terry said, placing his arms around Rhett's shoulders and giving him a kiss on the cheek. As if it had been planned beforehand, Terry, Emmy and Rhett left the bar.

'See you in about half an hour!' Rhett said, as the break-off group took its leave.

Caitlen bought another round of drinks and walked with Naomi over to Becky and Matt who were in earnest conversation.

'Are you joining us?' Caitlen asked Harriet and Gina, who were happily chatting away on adjacent bar stools.

'I think I'd better give Becky and Matt a wide berth, don't you agree?' said Harriet. 'It was alright when there were more of us sitting at the table, but that's a bit too intense for my liking.'

'Fair enough. Mind if we join you then?'

'Pull up a stool,' Gina replied. 'We were just chatting about Wes.'

'Really? It's amazing that they've given him a gig just like that.'

'Their next act has cancelled due to laryngitis. I think he saved them actually – the barman was telling me. He thought we were in for a double-dose of Lady Gaga, so Wes got his timing just right. He's a bit of a chancer that one, I said you needed to watch him.'

'I like him,' said Caitlen defensively. 'And he's got a singing voice to die for.'

Perfectly on cue, the speaker system fired into life.

'Ladies and gentlemen, it gives me great pleasure to welcome – for the very first time in Erin's Bar – the wonderful acoustic sounds of Mr Wes Nolasco, playing for you this evening the songs of James Blunt, David Gray, Ed Sheeran and more!'

There was polite applause, not quite as enthusiastic as it had been for the Queen covers band.

'I've been burned by his type before,' Gina continued. 'I was just warning Harriet off him. He's already pulled his special request move on her too. What was your song, Harry?'

'"Nine Crimes" by Damien Rice,' she replied. 'I love that song.'

'Thank you for giving me such a warm welcome at Erin's Bar!' Wes shouted confidently down the microphone. There was a big cheer from the crowd. 'It's great to be playing out here in Benidorm. Who's from the UK?'

There was another huge cheer.

'Wow, he knows exactly what he's doing,' Caitlen said, impressed by his presence on stage.

'I'd like to dedicate this first song sung in Erin's Bar to a very special lady in the audience. She knows who she is. This is "Babylon" by David Gray!'

There was another cheer from the audience, bigger and much more enthusiastic now.

'Yes,' Gina said, after taking a sip of her wine and looking earnestly at her new friends. 'He knows exactly what he's doing.'

FIFTEEN

Kasey and Harriet: May

'YOU LOOK like you got lucky last night!'

Kasey smiled as he stood up to hug Harriet.

'Well done on getting a table at this time of day,' she replied, avoiding the subject.

'Don't try and hide it from me. I can tell. You Brits are so stuck up most of the time that you can spot when you got laid a mile off.'

'I'd rather not talk about it,' Harriet said, 'and besides, I was hoping to have a chat about Caitlen's bombshell.'

Her Americano arrived, along with a square of brownie.

'I ordered for you when you texted to say you were on your way – perfect timing! I take it you're still leading with Americano?'

'The irony of this set-up isn't lost on me, you know. There's you, an American, with a pot of tea and a scone, and here I am, a true Brit, with my Americano and brownie. We're never happy with what we've got, are we?'

'You're in a pensive mood,' Kasey said, pouring his tea. 'What caused this? Bad date?'

'I'm not telling you who it was. I'd rather hear your thoughts on Caitlen's news. Do you think that'll be the end of our little group? It's been strained enough recently.'

Kasey folded down the lid of his laptop, placed the device in his bag and moved around the items on the table to create some more space.

'I can't say I'm not jealous,' he said after a while. 'Who couldn't use a windfall like that at our stage in life? But you can't knock her for it, it's a wonderful surprise.'

'I think she'll leave Terry,' Harriet picked up, eager to share her take on events. 'Did you see the way she was looking at him during the meal? I think he'll be history soon. He's a nice guy, but he doesn't really fit in, does he? I never understood why they ended up together.'

She bit into her brownie.

'Ah, chocolate! All I need to brighten up a dull morning at work.'

'I find Terry's gay references a bit tiresome,' said Kasey. 'It's like, get over it, Terry. I'm into men but I don't get excited about him being heterosexual every five minutes. I know he doesn't mean any harm by it but it stops me warming to the guy. He keeps putting this barrier between us. I wish he'd just forget the gay thing and talk to me as a mate. I should say something but I don't. I can't.'

Harriet sipped on her Americano.

'How long have you been here?'

'I got in just after nine. They're happy to let me sit and work as long as I buy drinks every so often. It's the joys of not having a boss. You get to sit in Starbucks all day and spend your evenings running backwards and forwards to the restroom because you drank so much tea.'

'Are you going to Spain? It's a lovely treat for us all. I thought that was really generous.'

'Of course I am. I wouldn't miss a free trip to Benidorm. I've never been before.'

Kasey's face suddenly changed.

'What?' Harriet asked.

'Nothing. You have a secret, I have a secret. We're allowed secrets from each other, right?'

'Yes, of course. If you tell me yours, I'll tell you mine. How do you work in these places, by the way. I couldn't concentrate with all this noise.'

'This is my office, darling. Besides, it's only packed like this at midday when you office drones file out for your lunch. It's you lot who make all the noise.'

'Ha, you're probably right about that, we're all desperate for our freedom. So, what's your secret?'

'Promise you'll tell me yours, Harry?'

'Yes, but it had better be a good one, because you've got to keep quiet about mine. I'm dying to share but you have to promise to keep it to yourself.'

'You're the sister I never had, Harriet. I'd trust you with my life. I'll go first. I have to tell somebody, it's pushed my blood pressure through the roof.'

Kasey had that look on his face again. Most of the time he seemed relaxed and approachable but recently Harriet had noticed a furrowed brow on more than one occasion.

'Go on then, you show me yours first.'

'You have to promise not to tell. This is serious, Harry. It's not gossip. I need your advice.'

'Promise,' Harriet replied, forgoing a second bite of her brownie. Kasey now had her undivided attention.

'You know I was moaning about Terry earlier? Well, it's

worse than that. The gay thing, I mean. He just uses that to tease me. Did you know he's bent?'

'What, you mean he's a bent copper?'

''Yes, that's exactly what I mean. I'm not supposed to be in the UK. I came over here to study and never went back.'

Harriet sat there and just looked at her friend. She'd never even thought about it. She'd known Kasey for several years and knew that he'd been a student but she had no knowledge about visas or any of the technicalities.

'How can you even do that?'

'I'm not proud of it, but it turned out to be quite easy. It's why I stay in that damned flat, though. The identity checks are so strict these days I daren't risk a move or it might be game over.'

'So how do you do anything? Banks and travel and stuff like that?'

'That's how I got in too deep.'

'Christ, Kasey, I can't believe you're telling me this. My little secret is nothing compared to this. Can they deport you?'

'I have forged documents. It was the most stupid thing I ever did. My name isn't Kasey, it's David, Davy when I lived in the US. It's why I work online – I keep my money in PayPal.'

The brownie was now unlikely to get eaten.

'Say something. I need to know you don't hate me.'

'I don't hate you, I'm just worried about what might happen to you. Does anybody need to know? There's not a problem until you get caught, is there?'

'That's why my blood pressure is so high. Terry knows. And he's holding it over me.'

'How the hell does Terry know? What business is it of his?'

'It turns out that he uses that police computer of his to check us all out. He says they all do it. He realised that Kasey Gaimer suddenly appeared from nowhere. He found a loose thread and couldn't stop unravelling it.'

'What did he say? Is he going to report you?'

'Worse. He's blackmailing me.'

'You're kidding me!'

'I don't know what to do. If I keep paying up, I can stay in the UK. The first payment is due just before we go to Spain. I'll be able to afford it, he won't bleed me dry. Maybe Cait's money will make the problem go away. Hopefully, he won't need the cash now.'

'Does she know about this? She'd be furious with him.'

'He told me if I shared it with anybody he'd have me sent back to the States, and he said it'll never come back to him because he'd fake a report from one of my neighbours so he would never be implicated. Imagine the shame of it, Harry. I don't even know what I'd do in the US. I've been gone years. I feel like a Brit now. I don't want to go.'

'I can't believe you're telling me this, Kasey.'

She took his hand and gave it a squeeze.

'We should have it out with him in Spain. We should tell him that I know what he's doing and that if he tries to blackmail you we'll snitch on him. If one of you falls, you both fall. Mutually assured destruction. How much money does he want?'

'That's the thing. It's not that much. He called it a contractual arrangement. He makes sure I stay in the UK in exchange for which I contract his services. He wants £200 a month. I can pay that, my small flat is so cheap.'

'Kasey, he's supposed to be your friend. He's supposed to be a friend to all of us. You can't let him behave like that.'

'When Caitlen told us about her money, I thought,

thank God, Terry won't need my cash anymore. But he's not said anything to me yet. And I don't want to bring it up. To be honest with you, I've just been burying my head in the sand.'

'We have to tackle this, Kasey. He's being a bully. He knows that you'll do anything to stay in the UK and he's pitched his blackmail money at a level that you'll be happy to pay forever. It's perfect for him. He knows you won't tell because you'll get sent back to the States if you do. But he's breaking the law, Kasey. He shouldn't have been snooping on you in the first place and he certainly shouldn't be black-mailing you. Promise me that we'll talk to him about it in Spain. And then, once we've sorted Terry out, you need to work with me to get your situation resolved. There are people connected to the council you can contact in confidence to see what your options are. You've got to dig your-self out of this lie. You're from the USA, we like you guys a lot, it can't be that difficult to sort out. Imagine what our attitude would be like if you came from Europe.'

Kasey didn't look like he was convinced, he needed time to think it through.

'Anyway, what's your secret? You promised you'd trade. It had better be good after what I just told you.'

'Alright, but you can't tell anybody, okay? It could cause mayhem.'

'Promise. What's so secret?'

'I'm still in love with Matt. He still loves me, he doesn't want to marry Becky. And we've been sleeping together again.'

Kasey laughed.

'Damn it, Harry, you'll have to do better than that for a secret. I knew it was Matt you'd slept with the moment you walked through that door. He's the only person who can put that smile back on your face.'

SIXTEEN

Benidorm: June

'ANYBODY UP FOR KARAOKE?' Gina asked. 'There's a bar up the road that does it. Very British, it'll suit Terry when the others rejoin us.'

'What's it called?' Caitlen replied. 'I'll text Rhett, he looked like he was still capable of answering his phone.'

'It's Curly's Tavern. All the Brits know it, they'll find it easily enough.'

The moment Wes had started to play Harriet's song, they'd decided to move on. Maybe he was being friendly, maybe not. He hadn't asked any of the men about their favourite song.

'Will Kasey get back from the hospital tonight or is he stuck with Porter?'

Harriet checked her phone for messages, but there was nothing.

'Emmy's going to be in the doghouse,' Naomi said. 'She just abandoned Porter. I reckon they'll be having words about that when he gets back – once Emmy has sobered up, of course.'

'I'm not sure if I've ever seen her like that,' Harriet replied. 'She likes her drink, but she's really letting her hair down. Terry doesn't help, they seem to bring out the worst in each other.'

Caitlen said nothing, but quietly clocked the comment. Her phone vibrated and she noticed that she was still set on UK time – she'd thought it automatically adjusted to Spanish time. She'd use part of her windfall to buy a new one.

'At least Rhett is reliable, Naomi. They'll meet up with us there. Apparently Emmy and Terry have overstayed their welcome at the heavy metal bar – they're both doing some pole dancing on the podiums at the moment. Can you imagine Terry pole dancing? I hope it's anchored into the ground properly or the whole building will come down.'

They left Erin's Bar with Wes still strumming away on the stage. Gina guided them along the street. There was shouting and raucous laughter coming from all directions, with couples, groups and individuals in various states of inebriation walking up and down the road.

'You should try the Old Town tomorrow,' said Gina. 'It's a bit more sedate if you like things that way. This is crazy Benidorm ... it's fun, though.'

Curly's Tavern was in full swing.

'Kasey just texted me,' Harriet announced as a tsunami of amplified music and the smell of beer washed over them. 'He's heading for the Old Town to find a gay bar and then he'll meet us back at the apartments. He's already dropped Porter off there. They've patched him up – it's nothing too serious, just some superficial burns.'

The music track ended, giving them respite to get some

drinks at the bar. Reluctantly Caitlen lined up another three bitters for Terry, Emmy and Rhett. There would be some bad heads the next day – they were all old enough to know better.

'Ladies and gentlemen, it's karaoke time!'

There was a big cheer in the bar.

'Told you,' Gina said. 'This is fun. Have you ever done karaoke, ladies?'

Naomi, Caitlen, Harriet and Becky looked at each other.

'Never!' they all agreed.

'Well, you haven't lived. How about we do a Spice Girls number just to warm you up? There are five of us. "Wannabe"?'

'You'll have to remind me about the zig-a-zig line, it's been a while,' Naomi laughed.

'They put the words on the screen. All we have to do is to decide which Spice Girl we're going to be.'

There was lots of laughter and, for the first time since they'd been in Spain, Caitlen began to get a feel of the fun they might have out there. This was why she'd invited everybody out for the trip. And Gina was proving to be an excellent guide.

As an old guy got up onto the stage and began singing, Gina wrote their names on the list.

'We're in between Neil Diamond and Britney Spears,' she said when she got back to the main group. 'Sounds like the one-night stand from hell.'

They'd divided out their Spice Girl names. It wasn't lost on Matt that Becky had ended up with Scary Spice. Naomi got Baby Spice, Gina was Sporty Spice, Caitlen was Posh Spice by virtue of her newfound cash and Harriet got Ginger Spice. As it turned out, things couldn't have been divided up more fairly, Harriet was even able to oblige on hair colour.

'I'm auburn, not ginger!' she protested.

'Yeah, but there isn't an Auburn Spice,' Caitlen had teased.

There was much amusement about the roles and the laughter grew to fever pitch as they shared their embarrassing Spice Girls memories.

Terry walked into the bar with Emmy and Rhett just as the Neil Diamond sound-a-like stepped up onto the stage to start performing "Love on the Rocks".

'Jesus, Emmy, you look totally drunk!' Caitlen said, concerned about the amount of alcohol her friend had consumed. 'Not everybody has a beer gut to store it in. Terry, take it easy with her, okay?'

'I'm fine,' Emmy reassured them, her speech slurred but still intelligible. 'I'll have a couple of soft drinks now. I'll be okay in no time.'

'That leaves a spare pint for me!' Terry said, downing one of the bitters that Caitlen had bought.

'Rubbish!' he shouted at the man on stage. 'Get him off!'

'Damn it, Terry, keep your voice down!' Matt urged. 'You'll cause a riot.'

There had been some backward glances from the crowd, it was clearly not the done thing to heckle the acts, even if they were tone-deaf.

'Neil Diamond should sue this guy,' Terry said, a little quieter this time around. 'It sounds like he just sat on a cat.'

'Hey mate, keep it down!'

A man twice Terry's size and with sleeve tattoos running up and down his muscular arms was looking annoyed.

'Terry, best be a bit quieter, eh? We don't want any trouble.'

It was Rhett who was appealing to him now. He knew that Terry had dealt with his fair share of arseholes during his time in the police and that the guy's size was unlikely to deter him, but Rhett wasn't so inebriated that he couldn't see who was to blame. Terry needed to pipe down.

Although the rendition of Neil Diamond's hit was unlikely to be a chart-topper, its melodic nature permitted a few minutes of conversation without having to shout over the noise from the PA system.

Caitlen was drawn by Matt's gaze. Becky seemed to have perked up. Being a part of the group that was going to have a go at karaoke had lifted her spirits and she was happily talking to Naomi. Matt looked pleased for the break, but he was now watching some guy chatting up Harriet at the bar. He had a face like thunder as the man gave her his patter and she laughed out loud at his jokes. Caitlen hadn't clocked that before. Was Matt still in love with Harry? That could make life difficult.

It was all over soon enough as the Neil Diamond song came to an end and the DJ announced that it was the turn of the 'Old Spice Girls' to perform "Wannabe". Polite clapping turned into an enthusiastic welcome as the inebriated audience realised they were being treated to the sight of five, non-pensioner women who, by and large, were in pretty good shape. They were certainly enough to give Neil Diamond look-a-like, seventy-year-old Len Davies from Leeds, a run for his money.

The first bars of the song began on the soundtrack and Gina led the way with the immortal opening words and before the first minute was up the five women were putting their hearts and souls into the performance. Nobody minded that the various Spices didn't seem to know who should be singing and when, neither that only one of them appeared to be able to dance in time with the music. It looked like a badly-rehearsed pop group made up of disobedient cats. But the entertainment value of Gina dancing like a pro – and the stunning sight of her in that dress – seemed to distract the crowd from the mayhem going on among the other members of the rapidly assembled pop group to her side.

Over at the bar were the three men, Matt, Rhett, and Terry, with Emmy at his side now sipping from a glass of orange juice.

The five Old Spice Girls were too caught up in their debut stage performance to notice anything else going on around them. But had they glanced over towards the bar, they would have seen some telling body language that might have predicted how things were going to play out over that short break in Benidorm.

As the crowd got with the flow of the choruses, Wes arrived, guitar in hand, fresh from his stint on stage at Erin's Bar. Although Caitlen had thought to tell him where they were moving on to, he was fed up with them. He'd gone through all the trouble of dedicating a couple of songs to the ladies, only to watch them walk out halfway through his David Gray number. And now here they were fooling around on stage in another bar.

Emmy was slipping her hands up Terry's T-shirt and stroking his back. They were engrossed in each other and their conversation.

Matt was ignoring Wes's moaning to Rhett, who was patiently listening and attempting to smooth things over.

Matt looked at Becky and Harriet on the stage, and then to the man just along the bar from him, the one who'd been chatting up Harriet. His eyes were riveted on her on the small stage, clearly waiting for his moment to intercept her once again as soon as they'd finished performing their number.

Matt looked between the Old Spice Girls. He wanted to switch band members. He wanted to be with Ginger Spice. But he wasn't the only man in that crowd who was determined to go home with Harriet that night.

SEVENTEEN

Benidorm: June

THERE WAS a huge round of applause as the backing track faded and the Old Spice Girls looked at each other on the stage and wondered what to do next.

Gina bowed and waved and the others followed suit.

'More!' came the calls.

The five women took a final semi-coordinated bow and left the stage.

'The Old Spice Girls, ladies and gentlemen!' the DJ announced. 'Weren't they amazing?'

There was another cheer, and the DJ moved on to introduce the next singer.

'Put your hands together for Britney Spears!'

The crowd had been suitably warmed up now, and gave an enthusiastic reception to the woman who was now stepping up onto the stage. She was well over sixty, but had the confidence of a regular karaoke performer.

'Jesus Christ, Britney Spears isn't wearing very well!'

Rhett announced, as the music started up again and the woman began to move on stage like she truly believed she was still the same age as Britney. 'You were great, ladies!' he continued. 'I didn't know you could sing like that, darling!'

Naomi was beaming at him.

'To be honest with you, neither did I.'

'Gina, you're amazing, where did you learn to dance like that?' Caitlen asked.

'Oh, thanks. Down the coast in Alicante. I joined a class there when I first moved out. I thought we did well for a debut performance.'

Harriet had been intercepted by the man at the bar and was sipping the cocktail he'd bought her. Matt watched while trying to get the gist of what Becky was saying to him.

'That was brilliant, Matt! You've got to try it. How about I put you and me down for a duet?'

'Yes, yes, whatever you want.'

She rushed off to write their names on the karaoke list. Harriet's new friend had popped off to the gents so Matt grasped his opportunity.

'You know he's got his eyes on you, don't you? He could have slipped anything into that drink of yours. It's not just teenagers who have to watch out for date-rape drugs, you know.'

'Look Matt, I'm a free agent right now. How do you think it makes me feel knowing that you'll be spending the night in the same bed with Becky? You know I want us to be an item, but I can't hang around forever. You need to end it with her or settle in for the long-term. You have to make your mind up, Matt.'

'And so I have to look on while this guy hits on you?'

'He's not hitting on me, he's just a good laugh. I have no

intention of sleeping with him. It's just a night out, we're probably going to a quieter bar when we've finished this drink. It's only a bit of company, Matt. You don't have to go all psycho on me. I can't stand here all night watching Becky pawing at you. I've got feelings invested in this, too, you know.'

'I'll do it, I promise. I just have to pick the right time. She's difficult, you know she is. Just give me some more time--'

'You alright mate?'

Harriet's companion was back. He'd immediately singled out Matt as a threat and had every intention of dispatching him fast.

'It's okay, he's a friend,' Harriet said. 'Matt's fiancée is over there, she was just on stage.'

The use of the word fiancée immediately reassured him, but in any case Matt was in no mood for a macho face-off. Besides, he would always lose. The only way a man like Matt could ever win a fight would be by sneaking up behind. He knew it too, and wasn't so stupid as to lock horns with this man. He returned to the main group, but continued to monitor their progress.

'So, anybody up for a re-run?' Gina asked. 'How about we put together a Boyzone or Take That group with the guys?'

'I've done enough singing for one night,' said Wes, drawing them back to his own performance. Gina wasn't taking the bait, but Naomi and Rhett were fast with the compliments.

'You were great up there, man. Sorry we couldn't stay, but you sounded awesome!'

'I hope you heard your dedications, ladies?' he asked.

Locked in conversation with her new companion,

Harriet couldn't hear him. He looked at Gina, but she didn't bite.

Becky came back.

'We're on after Elvis,' she beamed. 'I put us down for "You're The One That I Want". Hope that's okay?'

Matt gave a reluctant nod.

'Where the hell is Terry?' Caitlen asked. 'And Emmy? Did anybody see where they got to?'

There were blank looks all round.

'They probably went back to that heavy metal bar, that's much more their kind of thing.'

Elvis got up on the stage and began to sing "It's Now Or Never".

'We're up next!' Becky said to Matt, excitedly taking his hand. 'Make sure you cheer us when we go on, everyone.'

While they waited, excited at the prospect, Caitlen moved to one side to text Terry to find out where he'd gone. They'd only got the one key card for the apartment.

Elvis was mercifully brief, and Becky had Matt ready to jump back on the stage. He looked as if it was the last place he wanted to be.

'A big hand for Mike from Redhill!' the DJ said as Elvis departed the stage.

'And now, make some noise for Matt and Becky from Newcastle. These two love birds have only just got engaged, so let's make them feel welcome!'

There was a loud cheer and the opening bars of the song began.

Matt was first up. He looked like John Travolta on poppers. He nervously spoke the opening words of the song. His lacklustre delivery inspired an audible groan among the audience. That changed when Becky began to sing. At least there was something nice to admire in the form of an Olivia Newton-John lookalike.

Harriet finished her drink and turned to speak briefly to Naomi. She headed towards the door with her male companion.

Matt hadn't taken his eyes off her from the moment he'd stepped onto the low stage. He watched the body language. Whatever Harriet had told him, the man was intent on one thing. Would Harriet be able to resist?

Becky sang on but it was coming to the chorus, and it was clear to her that something was up. Her words ground to a halt at the beginning of her first line, leaving the crowd half singing along, half looking at each other in bemusement.

'Harriet, stop! I'm in love with you. I love you. Please don't go!'

'He wants to be singing KC and the Sunshine Band!' a man from the audience shouted drunkenly, before a hush descended on the full bar. Matt's words were amplified over the sound system.

'I'm ending it with Becky. I'm doing what you asked. Please don't walk out of that door!'

Sensing a moment, the DJ faded out the soundtrack. Even the stag party at the back had settled down and were watching the entertainment play out on the stage.

By the bar, Caitlen looked at Naomi in horror.

'What? What's going on?' Wes asked.

'Can't you see?' Gina scolded, impatient with him. 'Matt's in love with Harriet.'

'Damn it, I knew I should have started with Damien Rice,' he muttered.

'Seriously?' Gina replied tersely. 'Is that all you can

think about right now, Wes? You're a needy little shit, aren't you? And you're using Caitlen, too--'

'You bitch!' Becky shouted from the stage, making full use of the PA system.

There was a sharp intake of breath from the crowd.

'Looks like his chills are multiplying and he's about to lose control!' some wise-cracker shouted out.

'You can't leave him alone, can you, you little slut? You can't find anybody quite like him, can you? Does your casual shag over there know that you're damaged goods?'

'Really Matt, this is what you meant by picking the right time? You idiot!' Harriet shouted.

She was crying now, distressed not only at the way that he'd decided to declare his love, but also by the immense embarrassment of it having been done so publicly. She looked completely humiliated.

'Come on!' she said, taking the hand of the man she'd met at the bar. She stormed off, out of the club, into the Benidorm night.

'Harriet, wait!' Matt shouted after her, dropping his microphone on the ground and getting ready to exit the stage. Oblivious to the entranced crowd, he ran off after Harriet, followed by a crying Becky.

'We'd best head out after them,' Caitlen said. 'I've a feeling this is about to get even more ugly.'

They left the bar and there was silence for a few moments.

'Okay, sorry about that, ladies and gentlemen,' the DJ said. 'Let's get back to the karaoke. Here's Les once again, and this time he's singing David Soul's "Let's Have A Quiet Night In".

EIGHTEEN

Porter and Dr Barbara Lawrence: May

'HOW LONG HAVE you been having these dreams, Porter?'

Barbara Lawrence studied Porter's face, searching for any sign of agitation or stress. He remained calm, with his twitching thumb the only giveaway that what was coming out of his mouth and what was going on in his head were misaligned.

'Over three weeks now. I feel like the past has come back to haunt me. It's been so long since I thought about it. Now ... well, it's like I'm there again.'

'Have you told Emmy yet?'

His reaction betrayed the fact that he had not.

'You need to share what happened, Porter. It's a traumatic experience, it's been life-shaping for you. Emmy is your wife, you have to try harder to trust her. She accepts you for who you are.'

'Only, I'm not sure that she does, Dr Lawrence.'

She let that one hang. If she waited long enough he'd venture something else. The longer she waited, the more uncomfortable the silences became, and the closer she'd get to the truth. Even better, she was getting paid by the hour, so she still made money when they were saying nothing.

'I think she's having an affair. Either that, or she doesn't love me anymore. I'm not even certain that she ever did. She thinks I'm a fool.'

'Did you try the CBT exercises that we discussed?'

'You mean that cognitive behavioural stuff? I'm sorry, Dr Lawrence – and please excuse my language here – but it's a load of old bollocks.'

She was taken aback by that. Porter didn't swear as a rule. He was calm, thoughtful and considered. Profanity was how he gave a glimpse into his anger. She pushed ahead.

'For many people it can help them reroute their thought patterns based upon recurring and negative thoughts and create different behaviours--'

'I killed my brother, Dr Lawrence. You don't erase that memory with a bit of psychological mumbo jumbo. It doesn't go away if I play a CD of whale sounds or try to think happy thoughts when I picture his face.'

This is what she was looking for. For Porter, it always came back to the same thing. The world had moved on from the incident, but Porter was still stuck there, forever locked into his own memory of his teenage self.

'You were both high, Porter. You were only seventeen. It wasn't your fault, we've talked about this so many times. You even have the inquest to confirm it. It was an accident. You were not to blame.'

'But what happened afterwards, with Mum killing herself like that. It all followed from that night. She couldn't live without James, but she found it easy enough to leave me behind.'

Barbara Lawrence loved her job, but sometimes she saw glimpses in her patients which really scared her. Porter had been coming to see her for two years. He was a private patient, he had the money to keep paying the bills. She had people like him to thank for her new Tesla. Most of them were just bellyaching about childhood slights or petty life crises. Porter's issues were more deeply rooted, it made him both psychologically fascinating and an excellent source of recurring monthly income.

'Losing your mother at such a young stage in your life is bound to affect you. It's the person you need most choosing to end their life at a time when you're at your most fragile and vulnerable. But you can't blame yourself, Porter. It was your mother's choice to leave this world, it has nothing to do with you.'

'So why are the dreams back? I can see James's face so vividly ... he was grasping thin air. I wasn't too far away to reach out to him – he looked me directly in the eyes before he fell, as if he was blaming me for not being there for him.'

She watched Porter's eyes redden as he pictured his older brother falling from the wall of the multistorey car park. He'd told her before how they were high on pot, laughing their heads off, challenging each other to try out new parkour moves which were becoming increasingly dangerous. And then the inevitable happened. He could still hear the sound of James's head cracking on the pavement below, he'd told her.

'Have you been to the graves recently? Did you try my idea of writing them a letter to express how you feel about those events? You lost two of the most important people in your life within the space of a month. There's still a lot of pent up anger in there.'

'I'm going again after this appointment. I took the morning off work. I haven't written a letter – it feels stupid to me. But I'll say it in my head. I want to scream at both of them. I feel so guilty about that.'

'Don't. They left you without being able to say goodbye. You never got to sign out properly with them. You need to reconcile that.'

Dr Lawrence looked up at the clock.

'I think that's us for this session, Porter. You need to confide in your wife. You have to trust somebody else with this information. It's fine talking to me, I'm a safe person. But you have to trust other people – your wife, your friends. They won't judge you anywhere near as harshly as you judge yourself.'

AS PORTER WALKED out of Dr Lawrence's office, he thought about how much he enjoyed their chats. It allowed him to play out what was going on in his mind and speak it aloud. He hadn't told her everything; only he knew the full extent of it. One day he might trust her with that information. He was a man edging forward, working through a very serious realisation.

He'd chosen Barbara Lawrence because her office was close to the cemetery. He always went there after his appointment, it had become something of a ritual. He'd see Dr Lawrence, put flowers on the graves, then go for a coffee. Each time he did that it would allow him to relive the whole thing.

There was even a flower shop on the way to the cemetery. It was a small, local shop, the prices were almost reasonable. He bought a bunch of roses, then walked up the road into the sprawling graveyard. In spite of the cemetery seeming to get bigger every time he visited, Porter could navigate his way directly to the graves. They were looking older, the once pristine marble headstones now showing signs of weathering. He placed the roses on the graves, which were in adjacent plots. Even the ground had sunk now, there was no mound to show where the earth had once been displaced by the coffins.

Porter closed his eyes and thought back to that day. He was pissed with James. Not only was his brother able to fly through his exams without an ounce of effort, he also found teenage relationships easier than Porter and had his pick of the other female students. The truth was – and Porter knew it – he'd been insanely jealous of his brother. He loved him, of course, but at the same time he hated him. It was a resentment that had been festering for years. Their mum always gave James an easier time. Parents always say they love their kids equally, but Sarah didn't – after their dad left them, she clearly favoured James. He was less like their father, whereas Porter looked like a replica of him as he was when he was a young man.

He pictured the car park. They'd been with friends on the top floor, skateboarding down the ramps and terrifying any drivers who drove around the corner towards them. Eventually they'd tired of being hassled by angry motorists and decided to move on, but James had encouraged Porter to hang back.

'I got this joint at college,' he said excitedly. Porter could still hear his voice. 'Let's share it before we go home, I've never tried one before.'

They'd got silly very fast and started to dare each other.

Porter hadn't pre-planned it, he was as certain as he could be about that. It's why the sessions with Dr Lawrence helped, she allowed him to walk through it again and try to remember it correctly.

Had he encouraged James? When his brother had done that handstand on the highest wall of the car park, he had taken his life into his hands. Had it been the joint speaking when he challenged James to repeat the move and show him what he was made of? Or had he known in his heart that James would be badly injured or even die?

Even through his drugged-up haze Porter had noticed James stagger as he climbed up onto the wall. Yet he hadn't stopped him, he'd let him go ahead with it, even though he knew he was bound to fall. He thought back to how he'd walked closer to the wall in case James needed his help. As James moved into a handstand he lost his balance and desperately tried to steady himself. Had Porter moved forward, he could have offered a hand, he could easily have pulled James off the wall and into safety.

But a devil in him had taken over as he watched James struggle. He'd chosen not to reach out to pull him to safety. It had been a decision made in the heat of the moment. He loved his brother, yet something terrible in him had let him fall to his death. Porter had been struggling with this since the day he let James plunge to the ground. And standing there, eyes closed, after working through those events one more time with Dr Lawrence, he was becoming surer and surer of how he'd felt that day.

It had been exhilarating to watch someone on the cusp of death. To look into his brother's eyes and to know in that moment that he was God, only he could decide who lived and died. He wanted that feeling again – the terror, the absolute fear, the unique sense of power, and then the massive rush of adrenalin as you discovered that you'd got away with it, that the whole thing had been written off as a childish prank.

Porter didn't get much sense of power or control in his life. These feelings had only come back because of the way Emmy was making him feel so small and unwanted. It was like James and Sarah all over again, laughing at him, despising him. But Porter was beginning to build up the courage to experience that intoxicating sense of power once again. It was so close now, he could almost touch it.

NINETEEN

Benidorm: June

THEY SPILT out onto the street. Benidorm never seemed to sleep, there were people everywhere, drunk and boisterous, a stream of sweaty bodies.

'Which way did Harriet go?' said Caitlen, craning her neck to get a better view in the crowd. 'I'm worried about her with that chap, I don't want her doing anything reckless. What an oaf Matt was, doing that!'

'There's Matt over there ... Oh no, here comes Becky. Bloody hell, Cait, you certainly know how to screw up a good night!'

Caitlen looked at her sister, but had no time to reply. Becky was in tears, wild with fury at Matt.

'That bastard!' she screamed. 'He told me it was over between him and Harriet. And I believed him! I can't believe he did that--'

'Becky, try to calm down,' Naomi urged. 'You're upset –

of course you are – but let's find somewhere to sit down and talk about this.'

Wes had followed the small group out onto the street. He was trying to assess which way the wind was blowing. Gina too, a second newcomer, backed off, mostly concerned about Caitlen.

'Don't patronise me!' Becky screamed at Naomi, who retreated like she'd just dodged a scratching cat.

'They've headed up this road,' Rhett said. 'I can just see Harriet, and Matt's following them. Look, over there!'

He pointed to them in the crowd ahead. 'We should follow them. I'm worried about what Matt might do. Did you see the size of that guy Harriet's with?'

'Where the hell is Terry?' Caitlen asked. 'He's good at this sort of stuff, it's what he's spent his life sorting out fights as a copper. Domestics and drunkards. He's perfectly qualified for this.'

Gina put her arm around Caitlen.

'It's okay, Cait. It'll blow over. Let's make sure that Harriet's safe. Girl power, remember?'

She risked a smile and it calmed Caitlen immediately.

'You're right,' she said, then, 'Oh no!'

Becky had taken Rhett's coordinates and was running up the street like a scud missile seeking its target.

'Somebody stop her!' Caitlen said. 'She's in no fit state to have it out with Matt right now. Rhett, head Matt off at the pass. This is going to get even worse if they have this fight when they're all drunk.'

It was too late. Becky had spotted Matt and had run at him at great speed, jumping onto his back and punching him. It had taken him by surprise. He'd been following Harriet in the crowd.

'Get off me, you stupid cow!' he shouted, thrashing

around in the road and trying to throw her off. She was like a limpet and wouldn't budge. Her left arm was around his neck, she was punching his side with her right arm and digging her feet into the sides of his legs.

'Oh Jesus! They're gathering a crowd' said Caitlen.

A circle had formed around Becky and Matt, mainly of young men holding bottles and cheering on Becky.

'Give him a good thumping!'

'That's right luv, kick him in the nuts!'

'Can I get a turn, treacle?'

All of this seemed to spur Becky on in her fury.

'You lying, cheating bastard!' she screamed. 'You just couldn't leave that whore alone.'

Matt was tiring and she was hurting him. He lurched to one side and, caught completely off-guard, Becky fell off his back onto the pavement. There was a gasp as her head slammed onto the road. There was silence as she lay still in the street. Matt turned around to look at her.

'That was bang out of order, sunshine!' somebody said, and a fist slammed into his face. His legs weakened and he crashed to the ground. There was little concern for Matt, attention had now turned to Becky.

Rhett finally got to him.

'Damn Matt, are you alright?'

He was dazed, his nose filled with blood.

'That hurt like hell! I need to find Harriet. Where is she?'

'Steady Matt, you've just been punched in the face by a brick shithouse. We need to make sure you're okay.'

Matt staggered to his feet.

'I must see Harriet,' he said, running off again.

'That was not cool, man!' somebody shouted at him.

'Let him go,' Naomi said, catching up at last. Caitlen, Gina and Wes were close behind.

Becky was stirring on the pavement. She was perfectly alright, but enjoying the attention of the crowd. For a moment she forgot Matt as a group of young men crouched down around her to make sure she was okay. She sat up and looked around. Her friends were watching on. The fall to the ground had calmed her, she was tired now, her fury burned out for now.

Wes moved in and bent over her.

'Let me help you,' he said, offering his shoulder as a crutch. He shifted his guitar case into his left hand and made space for Becky.

'Do you know this guy?' somebody asked.

'Yes, it's fine, he's ... a friend. It's okay, thank you.'

Wes helped Becky to her feet and the crowd dispersed.

'You okay, Becky?' Naomi asked.

She nodded. Wes guided her over to a low wall outside one of the bars. The others joined her and they all sat in silence for a while.

'Should I go after Matt?' Rhett asked, looking at Naomi, then Caitlen.

'No, leave them,' Caitlen replied. 'Let them sort it out. Gina's right, it'll all blow over in the light of day.'

Becky's anger had changed to tears. Wes had his arm around her, ready to offer comfort wherever there was an opportunity.

'How about we go to that bar over there? They're serving coffees. We can sit down and chill for a bit.'

Becky nodded.

'Anybody joining us?' Wes asked.

'You go,' Naomi said. 'A bit of peace and quiet will do her good. We'll be over here if you need us.'

Wes walked over to the bar with Becky. They sat down at one of the outside tables and an attentive waiter came over to take their order. Caitlen watched as Wes moved a hand to wipe the tears from her eyes.

'He'll be asking her what her favourite song is next,' Gina said.

'Do you think so?' Caitlen replied. 'I'm just pleased he's with Becky. I'm not sure that I could deal with her right now. What a night this has turned out to be!'

'You can say that again,' said Naomi. 'Some holiday this is. You'd have been better off not being so tight-fisted and just giving us the money!'

'Naomi,' Rhett said, as if warning her off.

It was too late.

'And what do you mean by that?'

Caitlen sprang to her feet and turned to face her sister.

'Nothing. It's only that you've made a right mess of this holiday. We're all at each other's throats – you'd have been better off giving us a couple of thousand each. You've got enough money to last a lifetime, after all. God forbid you should fritter any of it away on us.'

'What's wrong with you, Naomi? I've only just found out about it myself. I don't even know what I'm going to do with it yet, let alone how I can help anybody else out. I thought you'd be happy for me, but all you can do is resent me for it. For once in your life can't you be pleased that I've had a bit of luck. It's about damn time!'

'All it's caused is trouble. Look at us all – you call this a holiday? It's already driven us apart and we've barely been here five minutes. If it wasn't for your bitcoin, none of this would have happened.'

'You think so? You think Matt and Harriet wouldn't have got together? You think Terry wouldn't still be an arsehole? You think you and me still wouldn't be at each other's throats like a couple of stupid schoolgirls? All this tension was here all the time, Naomi. We were always like this. The only thing the money has done is make everybody show their true colours. And it turns out my own sister is one of the biggest shits of them all.'

Naomi slapped her hard around the face. Caitlen was stunned. Rhett intervened.

'Okay, that's enough ladies. Naomi, come with me. We'll see you back at the apartments when we've all had time to cool off. She didn't mean it, Cait. I know you didn't mean it either.'

Rhett took Naomi's hand and walked her away. Caitlen didn't know whether to scream at her sister or cry.

Gina put her arm around her. It shook her out of her shocked state.

'It's okay, Caitlen. Everybody's just a bit highly charged tonight. Let them go off and give Naomi time to calm down.'

'Is this my fault?' Caitlen asked defensively. 'Did I create this mess? I was trying to do something nice for my friends. It's turned to crap.'

'It's not your fault, none of it is,' Gina reassured her.

'None of this would have happened if I'd kept my mouth shut and made a secret of it. Now I've gone and screwed everything up.'

'It's not your fault, honestly. People can be funny when it comes to money. You'd be surprised at how far they'd go to get their hands on it. It really does bring out the worst in people.'

TWENTY

Benidorm: June

'LET'S head for the Old Town and try and salvage the rest of the night. You could do with some cheering up.'

Caitlen looked over towards Wes and Becky. They were laughing now.

'Will she be okay with Wes, do you think? She can be a bit fragile at the best of times.'

'You know my thoughts about Wes, but to be honest with you he's probably just the kind of distraction Becky needs right now. Everybody's had a fair bit to drink. You lot are going to have to work through a lot of difficult conversations tomorrow morning – once you've slept off your hangovers.'

'I'm dreading it already. What made Naomi speak to me like that? We have our ups and downs – every sister does – but ... she seems to hate me. Did you see how angry she was? This money seems to have made everybody go crazy.'

'Let it go tonight. I know it's the last thing you want to do right now, but it's best left alone. Matt and Harriet will have to sort themselves out. Wes will take care of Becky – at least she'll get home safely. Rhett will talk Naomi down off the ledge. As for Porter, he's stuck with his sore backside!'

Caitlen burst out laughing.

'Oh, poor Porter. We shouldn't laugh. But he walks around sucking on that e-cigarette like he's a hi-tech Gandalf. Stuff like that always seems to happen to him.'

'He's married to Emmy, right? They are married?'

'Yes, I don't know why. Same as me and Terry. I guess sometimes relationships just … happen. You end up in one and sometimes wonder how you got there. Do you have anybody, Gina?'

There was a moment's silence.

'I'm sorry to pry, I didn't mean to. Don't answer that question unless you want to.'

'No, it's okay. Shall we start walking towards the Old Town, it's a bit of a walk from here, but it's well worth it. We can taxi back.'

They started walking.

'There's nobody special. I'll be honest with you, I like my life as it is. It seems to run quite well on its own without men.'

'Oh, you're not … are you?'

'No, at least I don't think so. I like men – but not all men. People like Wes … I know his type. I got hurt by one like him once. I guess it's made me a little more cautious. I have enough money, I'm not particularly interested in having kids. This life suits me. It's freedom I crave most.'

Caitlen felt the pang once again. It had started within five minutes of getting to know Gina. There was something about her which made Caitlen see the possibilities in her own life.

'Doesn't the beach look lovely at this time of night?' Gina asked.

'I love this place,' Caitlen replied. 'It's how it makes me feel – I love the sensations I get here, the warmth, the light and the breeze. It makes me feel alive ... free ... unburdened.'

'What about Terry?'

'Who knows?' Caitlen sighed. 'It just feels so difficult to end it. The house, the money, the fallout. I know that it has to be done, but I don't know when I can face it.'

'You don't have to go back home, you know.'

'What do you mean?'

'Well, who owns the house? Does it even matter? Naomi can move your stuff out. You could just stay over here. Break it off with Terry. You can use my spare room and we could work together while you get established. We'd have great fun!'

Caitlen looked out towards the sea and could just make out the dark shape of Peacock Island in the distance. To their right, the sounds of the bars and clubs, to their left the gentle swishing of waves kissing the golden sand of the beach.

'It's so tempting,' Caitlen replied, her mind drifting off into the possibilities. 'But I can't just abandon everybody. We at least need to get to the end of the week. It can't go much further downhill after tonight. I don't want it to end like this.'

'That's fair enough, but give it some thought.'

'I will. I need to get it all sorted out in my head. Naomi and I have a difficult day ahead of us tomorrow. I can't remember the last time we screamed at each other like that. We were both out of control.'

'Do you run?' Gina asked, out of the blue.

'Not much,' Caitlen replied, taken aback by the sudden change of topic.

'Come and jog along the beach with me. It's wonderful at this time of night. Feel the wind in your hair and the softness of the sand. I won't go fast, just a slow trot, I promise.'

Gina jumped over the short wall that separated the sand from the promenade and waved Caitlen over.

'What the hell!' Caitlen said, joining her friend on the sand.

'Over by the sea, the sand is wet there, it's easier to run.'

They took off their shoes and held them in their hands, setting off at a steady pace. With the sound of the bars and loud music now drowned out by the waves, Caitlen felt as if she was lost in another world. She experienced a new exhilaration and freedom. She began to run faster, the wind blowing her hair back, sometimes catching a wave and feeling the water splash up her legs. It made her feel alive with a vigour that had been rinsed out of her several years ago.

She reached the end of that part of the beach and stopped, breathless and sweating but elated.

'Where did you learn to jog like that?' Gina asked, struggling to regulate her breathing. 'You gave me a run for my money there.'

'I haven't run in years. It felt so right – I feel so good. How did you know that was just what I needed?'

'I've lived here a while. You'd be surprised what a run along the beach can do. Get your breath back, we're almost at the Old Town now. It's a bit of a climb to finish off with.'

In Gina's company it was all too easy to forget the life she had back in the UK. Gina knew the bars well, and the acoustic music was much more to Caitlen's taste, allowing them to speak and get to know each other better. By the time it was three o'clock in the morning, Caitlen was exhausted.

'They'll all be in bed now, right? I'll be able to sneak in without setting them all off?'

'I would think so,' Gina replied. 'You can stay over at my place if it's still sounding a bit lively. We'll sneak up the stairs – nobody will hear us if we're quiet. I'll sort us out a taxi.'

As they made their way through the lobby, Caitlen was feeling increasingly tense. Her bright idea of taking everybody on holiday had completely backfired on her. She wondered if things could ever be the same again. They took the stairs instead of the lift. As they neared their floor they heard sobbing – it sounded like a man.

'No chance of sneaking in then,' Gina whispered.

They walked up the final step into the hallway. Slumped outside Harriet's door was Matt weeping loudly, bloodied and exhausted, his head bowed. To his side, the door to Caitlen's apartment was slightly ajar.

'Are you okay?' Caitlen asked. Truth be told, she didn't really want to know.

'She's in there. With him!' he shouted.

'Shhh! You'll wake everybody up.'

'I'll take him into my place for a coffee,' Gina whispered. 'You coming?'

'I'll check the apartment first and let Terry know I'm back – and Naomi too. I might be angry with her, but I still want to make sure she's okay.'

Caitlen pushed the door open and walked into the

room. There were empty cans on the table and no sign of Rhett and Naomi. There was a groan from the couch, the unmistakable sound of Terry snorting in his sleep.

Caitlen moved towards the sofa to assess what state he was in. She peered over the back of it expecting to see a drunken Terry crashed out after a heavy night's drinking. She got more than she bargained for. Terry was lying naked with Emmy wrapped up in his arms, also with no clothes on.

'You bastard, Terry!' she shouted. 'I'm hanging on all this time trying to do the decent thing, and you're sleeping with Emmy. You're a piece of shit, Terry. You really are.'

She was furious, she saw straightaway that this had been going on under her nose all the time. She'd been agonising about how to end it and at any time the scumbag would have been happy for her to walk away.

Doors were opening along the hallway. Terry and Emmy were awake now. Emmy had grabbed a cushion to cover her modesty, Terry was seriously groggy from the beer. Porter had come out of his apartment along the corridor and was standing at the door in his boxer shorts, the top of his left leg bandaged.

'What on earth ... Emmy? For fuck's sake, Emmy, really? Is this what you were doing when I needed you in the hospital?'

Behind them, Harriet's apartment door opened.

'You alright, Caitlen. It sounds like somebody died out here.'

'These two ... these two have been sleeping together for God knows how long!'

Gina stepped out from across the corridor, closely followed by Matt who had been lured by the sound of Harriet's voice. He walked out of Gina's door directly into the path of the man Harriet had met earlier in the pub. While he was still taking in the situation, Becky emerged from the room they were supposed to be sharing at the other end of the hallway to be followed moments later by Wes wearing a pair of back-to-front boxers.

TWENTY-ONE

Caitlen and Luke: April

'DAMN, YOU LOOK GOOD!' Luke said, 'How do you do it? You look no different from when I last saw you.'

Caitlen gave him a warm hug and a peck on the cheek.

'You're not looking so bad yourself. You've lost a lot of weight. I don't mean to be rude, you know that never bothered me. It's just an observation. Are you working out or something?'

'Cycling!' he smiled. She'd missed that smile. It lit up his face. Terry's was more of a sneer.

'It suits you. You look lean and fit. If I didn't know better, I'd say you were at least five years younger.'

'I'll go out for a drink with you again any time, Cait. Nobody else flatters me like that.'

Luke indicated a free table and they sat down in the hotel bar. They ordered drinks and began to catch up on the years they'd lost since they last saw each other.

'We should have kept in touch, Cait, I'm sorry. It was

just too painful for me at the time. You know, I've regretted what we did ever since I left. Is it too late to say I'm sorry?'

The glasses of wine arrived. Caitlen took a sip, then held up her glass.

'Cheers, Luke! To our good fortune.'

'That sounds ominous,' he replied, chinking her glass.

'You brought the laptop, I take it?'

'Yes, I've got it. It's a good job you reminded me about it. It was still in my storage unit – it hasn't seen the light of day since I went to Thailand.'

His words brought Caitlen back to a time and a place: Luke's last day at work and the cake they'd made him, decorated with a sugar paste model of Luke lazing on the beach with his laptop. He went off to set up a digital business on his own but it had since gone bust. All it had taken was a bug in a corporate software rollout and his reputation was shot. Thousands, if not millions, of dollars were lost as a result, his career was over.

'Does it still work?'

'Yes, it powers up. I can't remember the password though. I thought you might be able to help with that. You used it almost as much as me when you were staying over.'

'I used to play *World of Warcraft: Cataclysm* on it, do you remember? It probably wouldn't be able to run a game like that now.'

There was a moment of silence as they thought back to how things had been. In spite of the horrible break-up and the fact that Luke had been a complete tosser at that time, it felt good to go back there. If they'd managed to end things better, she might not have run off into Terry's arms so readily. Luke and Terry were completely different. And Luke still had soft hands.

'It's great to see you, Cait, it really is. I didn't think

you'd ever speak to me again. You know, I didn't delete that old Hotmail account I had. I left it there with the specific aim of picking up any email you may or may not send me. I ditched that crock of shit email service years ago but I set up a forwarder ... just in case.'

'Good job you did, you're difficult to find online.'

'Yeah, I've gone dark. I had to close the business. I narrowly avoided bankruptcy. I've got just enough cash to hang on in there. I'm what actors would describe as resting – that means I haven't got a fucking clue what I'm going to do next. Sorry, you do still swear like a trooper, don't you?'

Caitlen laughed.

'In the right company,' she grinned at him, a gleam in her eye.

'So, what did you do after I headed off to Thailand like a filthy rat leaving you on your own to take care of your mum?'

'Mum died. I assume you know that.'

'I heard about it from Mike in the office. I sent flowers, but I didn't put my name on them in case you felt too angry with me. I'm sorry, Cait. I loved your mum.'

'So it was you who sent those flowers? We assumed the tag had got lost somewhere. Thank you, that was lovely.'

She reached out and touched his hand.

'Mum loved you, too. She was so upset about us going our separate ways. I think she blamed herself.'

'I should have stayed. You couldn't have left then – I know that now. But we were younger then and it felt as if there was no time to lose. I'm sorry, I shouldn't have pushed you. I should have supported you.'

'You don't need to keep saying sorry, Luke. It's water under the bridge. We make the best decisions that we can and usually they're a bit flawed. That's life, we have to live with it. The trick is to turn life's turds into gold.'

He laughed, leaving his hand where it was. It felt electric. She thought she'd never feel that touch again, not so welcoming and friendly. The last kiss she'd given Luke was tense and angry. It was a dismissal more than a display of affection.

'You still with Terry?' he asked. He'd been saving that question.

'Yes, I'm still with Terry.'

She watched his face drop.

'It's not going well, though. I think we're almost there with that particular relationship.'

'I'm sorry to hear that,' he said. He wasn't and she knew it.

'What happened? Did it run its course?'

'Life didn't really move on for me after you left,' she said, half to herself. She'd never said this out loud before.

'Mum died soon after you went to Thailand. I met Terry a couple of years after and we moved in together way too fast. It was good at first, I needed somebody who didn't remind me of ... I needed a change. But it wasn't going to last. Things changed at work, Terry was always distracted by his job and I ... I just became lost really. I've been stuck in a limbo of not daring to move. Things are pretty well the same as when I last saw you.'

'I'm sorry, Cait, really I am. Did you marry him?'

'No, we never married. No kids either. I think sometimes in a relationship you just know it's not right. If we'd married and had kids we'd have lost our ability to back out. I think subconsciously we both wanted to leave the exits open.'

'What will you do? What's your plan?'

'That's why I asked to see you. It just so happens it's rather timely that you're down on your luck.'

Luke took a sip of wine.

'Go on, tell me more.'

'Remember that Christmas when we were in the office on our own?'

'Do I remember that Christmas? We had sex in the staff kitchen. It was the only place without a CCTV camera. Do you remember trying to figure out where was safe?'

Caitlen had forgotten that part of the story. They were the only members of staff who'd been stupid enough not to book leave. They were a couple then, so they figured that they'd manage to pass the time pleasantly enough. Luke had started talking dirty to her, they'd got all hot and bothered and were desperate to find a place to have sex. They'd been frantically running around trying to figure out which areas weren't covered by cameras. It was either the toilets, the stationery cupboard or the staff kitchen. They'd had exciting, frantic sex on the round table in the corner of the kitchen. The same place where Mavis Nicholls ate her sandwiches every day. That made it feel even more naughty.

She'd never had sex with Terry like that. He approached lovemaking like a new cabinet which had to be assembled from a set of instructions: Part A fits alongside Part B, Part C slips into Part D. It was like a deathly version of the Karma Sutra, written by IKEA.

'Try LukeCait2011,' she said, trying to shake off the thought of it.

'What?'

'The password. LukeCait2011. Give it a try.'

Luke flipped open the lid on the old laptop. He typed in the password. It worked.

'Jeez Cait, how did you remember that?'

'Remember how we used to laugh about getting one of those sun strips in the car? The type where couples used to display their names? You don't see it anymore, but quite a lot of people did it in the old days. We always used to make our passwords with what we'd put on our imaginary sun strip. Plus the year that we created it. We broke up in 2012, you got that laptop in 2011, easy! Who needs Sherlock Holmes?'

'So what's on here that's so special? I can't even remember what's on this hard drive, it's probably full of all sorts of crap.'

'Do you remember that after we had sex we'd still got a full afternoon to kill? You never did take very long. Don't you remember our bet? The bitcoin one?'

'Damn, Cait, I'd forgotten all about that. Of course, we bought bitcoin, didn't we? Bloody hell, that was ages ago! It'll be worth a frigging fortune now.'

'Yup,' she nodded smugly. 'At current valuation, just short of half a million.'

'You're kidding? You're bloody kidding me, Cait?'

Luke tapped at the computer urgently, searching through his files.

'It's here, it's just a barcode and a long password key. Is that it? Is that enough to bring it back from the dead?'

'That's all you need, Luke. That's your private key to the bitcoin. We bought a hundred dollars each. It's worth a fortune now.'

Luke beamed at her.

'Damn it, Cait, why did I ever let you go? You just bring good stuff into my life. This is incredible, I can hardly believe it.'

He reached out to take her hands across the table.

'I'm sorry,' he said, gently releasing her hands. 'I forgot myself for a moment there.'

'It's okay,' she replied, looking deeply into his eyes, reading the signals. 'I like it, Luke. I've missed it. I miss you. Shall we get a room? There are too many CCTV cameras down here. You know how it is with the CCTV cameras.'

It felt good again to be wanted, really craved by a man. And those soft hands too, she loved the feel of smooth hands on her skin. In fact, she couldn't understand why she and Luke had ever let it slip away.

TWENTY-TWO

Benidorm: June

'CAITLEN, it's not what it looks like, luv!'

'It's exactly what it looks like, Terry. And will you please stop calling me luv? I feel like I'm trapped in a Carry On film. You've even got your own Barbara Windsor.'

Emmy had rushed off into the bathroom clutching her clothes. She'd missed her knickers which were resting on the coffee table in plain view of the assembled company. Within seconds, the entire situation descended into chaos. Caitlen was screaming at Terry. She was not so much angry that he'd been having an affair, she was more frustrated by the fact that she could have ended it with him at any time rather than having to agonise about the best exit point. In fact, the affair was a bit of a relief. Porter was banging at the bathroom door shouting at Emmy. If Caitlen hadn't been so preoccupied with Terry, she might have caught a ferocity in Porter's eyes which she'd never seen before.

'You damn slut!' he was calling. 'You think you're better

than me. You never sleep with me, and all the time you're screwing Terry! What's so wrong with me that makes Terry a better bet?'

Matt had taken a run at Harriet's companion and was now in the middle of his second fight of the night. Harriet was distressed, trying to separate the two men. There was no way Matt was coming off better in this exchange.

'It's not what you think, Matt. Nothing happened. We were just talking – honestly!'

Matt wasn't listening. Harriet's companion floored him with one punch. That set off Becky who was ecstatic at seeing her cheating fiancé getting what he deserved. She marched up the corridor in her dressing gown and spat on his unconscious body as it lay on the floor.

Gina watched Wes smirking at it all.

'And you can wipe that smirk off your face!' she yelled up the hallway. 'If it wasn't me or Harriet it had to be one of the other women in this group. You're a predator, Wes. I know your sort!'

It couldn't have been timed better. The door to the lift opened and there were Kasey, Naomi and Rhett. They'd stumbled across each other in the Old Town and had a great night out together. And now they'd walked into the first ten minutes of *Saving Private Ryan*. It was a war zone.

Naomi, who was completely worse for wear, immediately picked up where she'd left off with Caitlen. The only members of the group who weren't shouting, crying or unconscious were Kasey and Rhett. Rhett was sick by the lift, it pooled out across the corridor.

'I knew I shouldn't have drunk that last beer,' he slurred, slumping down on the floor.

'Enough!' Kasey shouted.

'It was sufficiently abrupt to stop everyone dead.

Caitlen, Naomi and Porter sensed the change of atmosphere in the corridor and ceased their shouting.

'That's enough, everybody! We're supposed to be friends, but we look like a bunch of a hooligans at a punch-up. We've all had too much to drink and emotions are running too high. We need to calm down.'

He spotted Matt out cold on the floor.

'Somebody needs to take care of Matt. He might be seriously hurt.'

'You're all a bunch of nutters!' Harriet's companion said.

He stormed off along the hallway, almost slipped on Rhett's vomit and tried to regain his dignity.

'Screw all of you!' he shouted, and ran off down the stairs, realising that waiting for the lift to come up to their floor would have further ruined any dramatic exit.

'Well, good riddance to him,' Kasey said, looking disapprovingly at Harriet. She was crying now and trying to rouse Matt.

'He seemed okay in the bar,' she sobbed. 'Nothing was going to happen. I just needed to get away from all this for the night.'

Caitlen and Naomi were standing at the door of their apartment. Terry had taken refuge in the bathroom with Emmy. Kasey was in charge now and they all realised it was for the best.

'Here's what's going to happen,' he began. 'Caitlen, you're sleeping with Gina tonight. Wes, you stay in my apartment. Get your clothes, for heaven's sake.'

Wes took the instruction.

'Emmy's in with Harriet, when she unlocks herself from the bathroom. Terry, Rhett and Naomi, you're in this apartment – that's if you two can stomach a night with Terry?'

'I knew about Terry and Emmy--' Naomi said, then stopped short. It had been an unspoken understanding that none of them would ever discuss that awkward encounter in the burger bar.

'You knew?' Caitlen seethed. 'And you didn't tell me. And you dared to say this was all my fault.'

Kasey walked towards her and gently took her arm.

'Enough Caitlen. We're tired and drunk, this will wait until tomorrow. Go with Gina.'

Caitlen walked over to Gina who placed her arm around her, guiding her out of the room.

'Becky, you're on your own, unless you want some company tonight. Maybe Naomi would stay with you?'

Naomi looked at Rhett, crashed out and sitting in a pool of his own vomit.

'I think that looks like a good bet,' she said, walking up the corridor. She stepped over Rhett, and went back to her room with Becky. Wes was still looking down the hallway from Kasey's doorway. Seeing that Becky was now out of play, he pulled the door shut.

'What about me?' Porter asked. 'I don't want to see that slut of a wife of mine ever again.'

'You've got your own room. Emmy's in with Harriet. How's your leg?'

'Sore. Really quite sore.'

'Go to bed, rest it. I'm sending Matt over to your room when he's sorted out.

Porter was exhausted and seemed grateful for the direction that he was getting. Like a chastened child, he made his way back to his apartment.

'What about Matt?' Harriet asked.

'For the second time this evening, I'm taking one of you to the hospital. He needs checking over, he's still out cold.

That must have been quite a thump. What were you think-ing, Harriet? We all know that Matt's still in love with you. How did you think it would end?'

'I'm sorry. I wanted to take my mind off him. It's been torture seeing him with Becky. I wasn't going to sleep with that guy. He just made me laugh. I needed it.'

'Go to bed,' Kasey said.

'You promise you'll take care of him?' she asked.

Kasey nodded. Harriet walked into her apartment.

'I'll leave the door ajar,' she said. 'Tell Emmy to make herself comfortable whenever she comes out of the bathroom.'

Kasey had successfully herded the flock of errant sheep and separated the hostile parties.

He walked into Caitlen's apartment and banged on the bathroom door. Kasey heard the sound of the lock being slid across and the door started to inch open. Terry peered outside, as if scared of being lynched.

'Did you have to do this on holiday?' Kasey asked. 'She bought this as a treat for all of us and this is how you thank her. You and me need to have a serious conversation, Terry. Everything stops here. Everything, you understand?'

'What's he talking about?' Emmy asked.

'It's nothing, Ems,' Terry said. 'Just something me and Kasey need to sort out.'

'It'll wait until tomorrow,' Kasey said. 'We'll wait until we've all slept it off. Terry, sort out Rhett and make sure he gets to bed safely.'

'But--' Terry began.

'I don't think now is the time to be causing problems, do you Terry?'

Terry stopped talking and stepped out into the corridor.

'Jesus, I'm not clearing up that mess--'

'Terry!' Kasey snapped.

'Okay, okay,' he said, resentfully making his way towards Rhett.

'Emmy, you're in with Harriet. Stay away from Terry and Caitlen for a while. I need to figure out how to sort this out and get everybody talking again. Just steer clear for a while, okay? Stay with Harriet.'

He escorted Emmy to Harriet's door and helped her over Matt's crumpled body.

Terry was manoeuvring Rhett along the hallway, a look of disgust on his face.

'Make sure that vomit gets mopped up before you crash out. And wait in your room until I decide what to do with everybody.'

Terry muttered under his breath.

'You got that, Terry?'

'I got it,' Terry said. 'Don't worry, I feel like right now I could sleep forever.'

Matt was stirring. He opened his eyes and looked up at Kasey, struggling to find his focus.

'Damn, my head feels like it was hit by a hammer. What's been going on?' he asked.

'Oh, nothing much,' Kasey said, his voice dripping in sarcasm. 'It's only a bunch of friends who want to kill each other, that's all.'

TWENTY-THREE

Benidorm: June

CAITLEN WAS WOKEN up early by her phone beeping. It was a text from Kasey.

'Poor Kasey must have been up all night clearing up our mess.'

Gina was next to her, they'd gone to sleep side by side in her double bed. Neither of them could be bothered to make up the bed in the spare room.

'What does he say?' Gina asked, rubbing her eyes. 'What time is it? I don't usually sleep in this late.'

'Just past seven, according to my phone, so eight o'clock Benidorm time.' Caitlen replied. 'Kasey wants us to disappear for the day. He says he's sending us all off at staggered times. He wants us all to keep apart and think through what happened. He's booking a table at a restaurant tonight. He wants us to thrash it all out there.'

'Seems like a good idea, although I'm not sure how you

all move on after that shitstorm. I've never seen a bust-up like that before. And you're all friends you say?'

Caitlen chuckled.

'We're supposed to be. I thought this holiday would be a treat for everybody. I'm beginning to think it was all my fault, like Naomi said. If I'd kept quiet about the money, none of this would have happened.'

'You're not to blame,' Gina said, touching her arm. 'Your friends decide how they react to your money, not you. You can't control that. You've done a decent thing here, Caitlen. They should be grateful that you paid for this trip.'

'But that's just it, isn't it? Nobody wants to feel they're accepting charity. Really, all that everybody wants is to get their hands on the money for themselves. It just creates jealousy. I should have kept my mouth shut.'

'I was right about Wes, though, wasn't I? He was straight in there with Becky. Talk about an opportunist.'

'If it takes the heat off for Matt and Harriet, it's probably not a bad thing. At least it gives Matt some moral high ground. What a mess, Gina. I don't know how we're all going to move on from this.'

'Let's get started by having a shower and getting ourselves lost for the day. I'll show you some of the sights. What do you think?'

'Yes, let's do that. I can't think of a better plan than Kasey's. I have no appetite to see Terry or Naomi at the moment. Besides, they were all pretty drunk. There's no point in trying to talk when everyone's got a hangover. Kasey says in his text we have to be out by 8.45 at the latest. He's sending Wes off next, he doesn't want any of us to see each other. Best thing, I reckon.'

Caitlen and Gina took turns in the shower, leaving the apartment door ajar so they could hear if there was any movement along the corridor. Everything was quiet. They slipped out at half-past eight and Caitlen texted Kasey to let him know the coast was clear.

'Are you alright in my T-shirt? I think we're pretty well the same size.'

'I think you're being kind, Gina. I'm sure I'm two sizes up from you and this is one that you use as a nightshirt. But thank you, yes, this is great. Better than the one I had on last night.'

After such a terrible night, Caitlen was surprised to feel so enthusiastic about the day. There would be the reckoning at the evening meal, but that was twelve hours away. The sun was already burning fiercely, the sea was sparkling, and the long sands looked like a path of gold. The sky was an invigorating blue and she had her new friend with her. There was no baggage to worry about for the time being.

'You are going up to the Cross before you leave, aren't you?' Gina asked.

'I think we might be burying a few bodies up there before the week is done!' Caitlen laughed. 'How about Terry for starters?'

'Shall we have breakfast here?' Gina asked. 'It's a great view of Peacock Island.'

They pulled up wicker chairs at one of the free tables and ordered fresh orange juices and a couple of fry-ups.

'I know what Terry did must hurt, but it's for the best in the long run. It gives you the upper hand now and you can move on.'

'Yes, but with Emmy? I thought she was a friend. I thought all of them were my friends. I suppose it makes sense, though. They're always running into each other on crime scenes. They always got on well. I just can't believe it was happening under my nose. Still, what is it they say about people in glass houses?'

'You haven't, have you?' Gina asked, intrigued.

'I haven't been totally honest with you. In fact, I haven't been totally honest with anybody. I'm as bad as all the rest of them.'

The orange juices arrived and Caitlen took a long sip.

'There's nothing like freshly squeezed orange juice to wash all the morning crap out of your mouth.'

'Carry on,' Gina said. 'You can't leave me hanging like that.'

'I cheated on Terry a couple of weeks ago. Only once. Well, twice in one sitting actually. But you know what I mean, it counts as once.'

'You're kidding?' Who with?'

'You know the guy I bought the bitcoin with – Luke? I met up with him to see if he still had his hundred dollar purchase. He had. We used to be an item. What do they say on Facebook? It's complicated. Well, it turns out it's not so complicated for me and Luke. We're almost bitcoin millionaires between us and we've still got a good thing going on. As soon as I sort out the Terry situation, we're going to give it another try.'

'Hellfire, Caitlen, you're all as bad as each other. I used to watch EastEnders when I lived in the UK. You lot make it seem like a cosy sitcom by comparison. I can't believe you!'

The fry-ups arrived. Caitlen dipped her bacon into her egg and put the first forkful into her mouth.

'There's nothing quite like a fry-up, even when you're abroad. You can't beat it! I don't feel happy about what I did with Luke, Gina. But it still felt right. I half did the decent thing. I told him it mustn't happen again until I've sorted things out with Terry. We did have sex one more time after that, but as I say, it doesn't really count as it was on the same day.'

'Wow, and I came to Benidorm for a quiet life,' Gina smiled. 'I'm not judging, by the way. Sometimes life events occur in the wrong order. I get it. As you said, Let she who is without sin ... and all that. Are you alright there? You look like you're having bra trouble.'

Caitlen was feeling around under her T-shirt. She was so agitated a group of young guys sitting across from them had noticed and were watching to see if the T-shirt was going to come up any higher.

It did. Caitlen pulled it right up, revealing her cleavage and bright blue bra. She moved her hand around her breasts, her face white now.

'I've lost it. I've lost the bloody bitcoin thing!'

'You're messing around, aren't you? I thought you had it taped inside the cup. Here, let me check.'

Gina leaned over and put her hand up Caitlen's T-shirt feeling all around the cup. There were cheers from the table of lads.

'I've paid to see worse sex shows than this!' one of them called over.

After a few minutes of frantic searching, Gina stopped and looked at Caitlen.

'Damn, Caitlen. It's not there. That thing has almost half a million dollars on it. Think, Caitlen, where could it be?'

TWENTY-FOUR

Becky and Wes: June

'LOOK AT THEM, they've parked me with you and now they're happy to buzz off into the night and leave me. Some friends they are!'

Becky sipped her coffee and wiped the tears from her eyes.

'I bet I look a mess. Has my mascara run?'

'You look just great,' Wes said, taking a packet of tissues from his pocket and handing one to Becky.

'Here, take this. Just wipe under your right eye, then you're fine.'

She started to dab in the wrong place.

'Here, let me,' Wes said, gently taking the tissue and wiping away the blotch of mascara.

'There, good as new!' he smiled. 'That was some show your boyfriend put on up there,' he said. They were sitting outside the café bar, watching their friends heading back into the nightlife after one of the biggest bust-ups Wes could ever recall seeing.

'I don't want to interfere, but he was well out of order doing that in front of all those people. What an embarrassment for you.'

'He's my fiancé,' Becky sniffed. She blew her nose on the tissue and repositioned herself in her chair. 'I'm furious with him. What a humiliation. I feel worn out by everything, I feel like I want to crawl under a rock and sleep forever.'

'It takes it out of you, a row like that.'

'I thought they were my friends. When we were up there on stage, doing the Spice Girls thing ... Did you see us? It was great fun. Then, all of a sudden, Matt does that.'

Wes moved his hand across the table to touch her arm. Becky was so self-absorbed that she barely noticed it.

'What will happen now? With Matt, I mean. Do you think he'll make it up with you?'

'No, the little rat always loved Harriet. I should have known it. I thought I could win him over, but she's like a rash. Once you've got it you can't get rid of it. I could kill him, honestly I could.'

'Relationships, eh? Can't live with them, can't live without them!'

'What about you, Wes? What's your story? We know very little about you other than that you play guitar and move around a lot. Is there anyone in your life?'

This was uncomfortable ground for Wes. He preferred to talk about other people. It kept the spotlight well away from him.

'I'm a free spirit. There was someone special ... but, well, that didn't work out for me. And so I'm a wanderer, I travel the globe and wherever I lay my hat, that's my home.'

'You were good on stage tonight. Being a performer must be handy for meeting people.'

'Yes, it's great. You meet all sorts of people doing what I do. Some of them good, some of them trouble, if you know what I mean.'

Becky didn't know what he meant, but she dismissed it as a figure of speech. There was an awkward silence. Neither of them had really thought things through beyond her calming down and getting away from the immediate stress of the fight in the street.

'How's your head? It looks sore, we should get that looked at. Does it hurt?'

Becky felt the back of her head.

'Ooh, there's a bump. Is it bloody? It feels a bit wet back there.'

Wes gently placed his fingers on her head and gingerly moved them through her hair.

'That feels nasty. Any double vision or anything like that?'

'It was a bit of a crack when I fell on the pavement, but it's nothing a paracetamol or two won't sort out. There's one of those flashing green crosses at the end of the road. Can you see it? That's a pharmacist, isn't it? Shall we see if it's open?'

'Good idea. Maybe we can get some antiseptic there too, and I can clean it up for you.'

'Thanks Wes, I appreciate it. It comes to something when the people who are supposed to be your mates abandon you with someone you've barely met and he turns out to be the kindest one out of the lot!'

'It's my pleasure – anything I can do to help.'

They drank up their coffees and Wes left a five euro note tucked under his cup.

'Thanks for paying,' Becky said. 'I haven't got any money on me. Cait's paying for everything.'

'They paid me in cash this evening after I'd done my session. It was good money, so my treat.'

Wes held out his arm as he stood up to leave. Becky took up the offer and placed her hand on his biceps.

'Blimey! You work out!'

'Ha, yes. I have to keep in shape for my stage work.'

Wes was pleased that she'd noticed. He picked up his guitar case with his left hand and they made their way up the street towards the pharmacy.

'What's the deal with Caitlen?' he asked. 'She's very generous, but why is she paying for everything? Has she won the lottery?'

'Something like that!' Becky laughed, feeling the tensing of his biceps as they established a steady walking rhythm.

'Have you heard of bitcoin?' she asked.

'I don't know much, but I do know that some people have got very rich from it. Why?'

'She has bitcoin. She bought it several years ago and now it's worth a fortune.'

'Wow, lucky Caitlen. How much is she worth?'

'Almost half a million dollars – or pounds – I can't remember which.'

She felt Wes's biceps tense hard when she said that. For a few seconds, they were rock solid.

'Either way, it's a lot of money. This holiday was supposed to be a big treat for us all. Look how it turned out.'

'How do you even spend bitcoin? Do you keep it in your wallet?'

Wes was immediately interested in the topic.

'I know very little about it. Other than that it's not like

real money. The reason we're all here is that she shared out her passwords with us. I've got two words to remember: *pasta* and *shipwreck*. It's crazy stuff, she had this big master password made up of lots of random words. And that's how she gets her hands on all that cash. Oh, and she has some USB drive or bitcoin gadget which she keeps all the digital money on. You can't get at it unless you have the full code. It's crazy, if you ask me. Your money is much safer in the bank.'

'Wow, it seems mad. So, I assume those two words that you have are useless without everybody else's. Is that right?'

'Yes, but here's the thing. Can you keep a secret, Wes? I'm not proud of myself for this.'

'Yes, of course I can, Becky. You've had a tough enough night already. I'm not going to make it worse by sharing your deepest, darkest secrets.'

'When Matt and I were going to get married--'

She stopped dead in the street.

'I guess that's not happening now, is it? The bastard!'

Sensing that Becky was about to head off at a tangent, Wes diverted her.

'Look, the pharmacy is shut, but there's a supermarket across the street. They'll stock a basic first-aid kit. What were you saying about the bitcoin?'

They continued walking towards the supermarket.

'Oh yes, I was saying I'm not proud of it but I took a photo of all her passwords. We were at her house and she was sharing them out privately. She just left this big list of them on the table. I couldn't resist it. I was angry with her at first, I wanted her to offer to contribute to the wedding. Well, I don't need to worry about that any more. I can't believe I actually suggested to Matt that we should steal some of it. Can you believe that? I must have missed my meds that day.'

'You mean you can actually get your hands on all that cash with just Caitlen's USB device and the list of passwords?'

'Yes! It's remarkable, isn't it? She's terrified she'll lose it all. Who the hell wants to buy bitcoin if it's that unsafe? I'll stick with the banks thank you, at least you know where you are with them. What's the occasional financial crash between friends?'

They entered the supermarket. It was quiet and they were able to locate what they were after straightaway.

'Here, cotton wool, disinfectant and plasters. Everything we need.'

'Are you sure you're okay to pay for it, Wes? It seems a shame to spend the money you just earned on something as stupid as this.'

'It's no problem, Becky, honestly. I'm really enjoying our time together. Do you still have that photo?'

'Yes, it's on my phone.'

Becky touched the pocket of her jacket.

'I should delete it really, I shouldn't have taken it. Poor old Cait thinks she's created her own Fort Knox and here I am wandering around with the keys to the castle. It appeals to the devil in me, though. All those fools desperately trying to remember their bit of the password to protect Caitlen from some Russian hacker or massive heist, and here I am with the key to all of it. It's ludicrous. Caitlen should know better. Talk about misplaced trust. I reckon if push came to shove, we'd all steal her money if we could.'

'Don't delete that photo for now,' Wes said, paying for the first aid kit at the counter. 'We should show it to Caitlen, maybe give her a fright. It might encourage her to take more care. I mean, at least she can trust you. Imagine if it fell into the hands of someone she couldn't trust?'

Wes was keen to change the subject after they left the supermarket. He got her talking about Matt again and the anger was back straightaway, all thought of the bitcoin and the photograph long gone.

As Becky raged about Matt's treachery and described in detail the things that she'd like to do to punish him and Harriet, Wes's mind was somewhere else. All he could think about was Caitlen and her incredible good fortune.

TWENTY-FIVE

Benidorm: June

'WHERE HAVE WE BEEN? Perhaps it slipped out of my bra. Do you know if I'll still be able to get my money without it, Gina?'

'Yes, but you have to use your secret code. I hope you trust your friends because you're going to need those passwords back now. The full set of codewords is the only thing that can recover your money if you've lost the device.'

'The only time I left my bra ... damn, it was hanging off the back of your sofa while I was showering. I took it off last night before I went to bed. I didn't even think to check it, my mind was elsewhere.'

'Well, I haven't got it. It was perfectly safe in my apartment. Maybe it fell onto the floor?'

'I'd have seen it, surely? Didn't we leave the door ajar in case there was any movement from the others out in the corridor.'

'Damn it, Caitlen. I don't think anyone could have

found it in that time. I was getting dressed in the bedroom while you showered. It can only have been unattended for five minutes.'

'I sure as hell need those passwords from everybody now, but will the buggers let me have their secret words after everything that's happened? They probably hate me so much, they won't tell me just to be spiteful.'

'We should retrace our steps and make sure it didn't fall out in the street. Is there any chance of that, do you think?'

'Hello darlin', can uzz get yooz both a coffee?'

One of the guys who'd been entertained by the bra searching had come over to chance his luck.

'Piss off!' Caitlen screamed at him.

'Jesus luv, I didn't know yooz were both together!'

Caitlen stood up, furious now and stared angrily into his eyes.

'Shut the fuck up with the luv stuff. Just because I don't want to shag a spotty, greasy dickhead of a man who thinks a woman checking her bra is a come-on to everybody with a pair of balls does not make me a lesbian. Alright!'

'Yeah, yeah, sure luv.'

He backed off and returned to the table.

There were sniggers and Caitlen caught the tail end of a 'time of the month' comment. It wasn't the best time to test her. She was feeling furious enough at her own stupidity, losing the precious device. She could see her new fortune going up in flames. So when she heard the comment, the chuckling idiots were just the target she needed to vent. Before Gina could stop her, she ran towards their low wicker table – on it were eight pint glasses and various discarded plates covered with the debris from the morning's fry-ups – and she flipped it over, sending everything crashing to the ground.

'And this is what happens when a woman is on her period and she has to listen to a bunch of tossers like you sniggering away.'

Caitlen's face was pressed right up to the man's, as if it was a face-off. Observing the owner of the establishment head directly for the phone, the group of young men backed down. They each quickly placed a ten euro note on the table next to theirs and made their exit.

Caitlen was charged with adrenalin, but seeing them walk away made her burst into tears. Gina walked over to her, stunned at what she'd just witnessed.

'Hell, Caitlen, remind me never to piss you off. I take it you're not really on your period, by the way? You never get to see scenes like that in the Bodyform adverts, do you?'

Caitlen burst out laughing, a stream of mucus shooting out as she half-cried and half-shrieked. This is why she loved this woman. Gina was just the type of friend she needed in her life. Her new life. The one she'd just screwed over because she couldn't keep a small electronic device safe.

A police car drew up outside the beachfront bar.

'Shit, Cait, that's for you, I think.'

Caitlen's focus had been entirely on her immediate environment. It was only when Gina said those words that she began to take in the impact of what she'd done. For starters, there was the mess on the floor. Several of the older people had stood up and backed away, scared that they were about to witness violence of some sort. The owner was used to English idiots kicking off on the beachfront, so he had the local police on speed dial.

'Oh, I am so sorry everybody ...'

Caitlen looked around, horrified at what people must be thinking.

She moved towards the upturned table to start clearing up, but one of the police officers took her by the arm. The second officer was speaking to the owner, who was pointing in her direction.

'It'll be alright, Cait. Don't worry, they'll just take you to the station.'

Caitlen nodded, aware now that she would have to take any punishment on the chin. Gina spoke to the first officer.

'English, por favor?'

He shook his head.

'You go to the station with them. I'll find an interpreter, and I'll settle up with the owner and pay for the damage. It'll be okay, Caitlen, honestly. They'll just do the paperwork and you'll be on your way. I'll meet you at the police station.'

Caitlen was crying again now. She despised herself for what she'd just done. The thought that people might have been scared of her appalled her. The damage she'd done to somebody else's property was unforgivable. How could she have been so foolish?

'I'll pay you back for the damage, Gina,' she said as she was guided over to the police car. 'And please pay for everybody's food and leave a big tip, too. And say sorry to the owner--'

The car door was slammed before she could finish off her list. Gina had got the gist. Caitlen was sorry.

The second police officer had closed his notebook and looked like he was finishing off with the owner. Gina tried her luck again.

'English por favor?'

She was quite capable of dealing with everyday Spanish requirements, but lacked the linguistic confidence to shoot for a legal conversation in Spanish.

'A little,' the owner said, as the second officer shrugged.

'Will you press charges?' she asked.

The owner shrugged, he didn't understand what she was asking.

'Will my friend be in a lot of trouble?' she rephrased. 'We would like to apologise and give you some euros.'

'It is okay,' the owner continued. He explained something in Spanish to the officer, who nodded.

'Your friend is ... how do you say it ... sad, I can see. The policeman he must write the papers ... do you understand?'

'Do the paperwork. Yes, I understand.'

'But she will not be in trouble, she is very sad ... upset, I think you say. I can see.'

'Thank you,' Gina said, touching his arm and grateful for his compassion. 'I will come back today with some money to pay you for all this ...' She gesticulated to make it clear what she meant. 'I have sixty-four euros now. Let me pay for all these meals,' she continued, speaking much louder now. There were about eight people in the beachfront area and she reckoned that would take care of most of it.

There were murmurs of approval all round. Only the English would consider a free morning coffee a fair exchange for a fight breaking out right next to their table.

Gina shook the hand of the owner, handed him the euros, thanked him profusely, then walked over to assist the waiter who'd come out to start clearing up the mess. The police officer surveyed the scene, exchanged a few words with the owner and walked over to the car. Caitlen was staring through the rear window, looking very sorry for herself. She gave a half-hearted wave to Gina as the car moved off.

'Where is the police station?' Gina asked.

The owner gave her directions and she was relieved that it was a reasonable walking distance. It was not a service she'd had to engage with since arriving in Benidorm. Having managed to put the table back and assisted with clearing up the mess, Gina was about to leave the bar when she noticed that Caitlen had left her phone at their table.

She walked over to pick it up and put it somewhere safe. She did a double-take when she noticed what time it was, then saw that Caitlen had not yet adjusted the time to take account of the one hour difference with the UK. The phone was still unlocked, so she opened up the settings to change it to display the correct Spanish time. Not wanting to interfere any more, she locked the phone so that it couldn't be tampered with any further. She couldn't believe that Caitlen had put up with it like that for so long, but she was pleased to be able to put it right for her new friend.

As she walked along the beachfront, she pulled out her own phone and found the number of an interpreter that she'd used on a couple of occasions to sort out the contract on her apartment and take care of a few basic banking issues. Fortunately, he was available and Gina arranged to meet him at the police station. They'd have Caitlen out of there in no time, he reassured her. She'd get a rap on the knuckles, a short cool-off time in the cells, and she'd be out of there by mid-afternoon.

It was a twenty-five minute uphill walk to the police station, but Gina reckoned she'd manage it in twenty if she got a move on. She knew how anxious Caitlen must be feeling with all those Spanish voices and little idea what was going on around her. She took a left turn off the beachfront to begin her journey, winding across the town to her destination. The streets were busy and the sun was strong overhead, threatening a punishing day of heat and brightness.

It was not so busy, though, that she didn't do a double-take as she walked across the road from one of the many large Chinese bazaars that lined the resort's streets. He was wearing a cap and sunglasses, but it was the broad muscular shoulders that she recognised rather than the face. It was Wes, and he seemed to be out early spending his first wages from Erin's Bar. By the look of it his bags were filled with all sorts of new purchases. He looked like he was getting ready to go somewhere.

TWENTY-SIX

Benidorm: June

'I'M SO embarrassed about the whole episode, I just want the ground to swallow me up.'

Kasey squeezed Caitlen's arm. Harriet felt compelled to come in and give her a hug.

'I'm so grateful to you for sorting everything out, Gina. You've been such a gem out here, a true friend. That interpreter fellow was great. I hadn't got a clue what he was saying, but they released me fast enough.'

'Will there be any repercussions?' Kasey asked.

'What, other than being on Benidorm's Most Wanted list?' Gina laughed. 'No, she's safe, the owner was ecstatic that we'd gone out of our way to pay him for the damage and said we're welcome back any time. Can you believe it? The Incredible Hulk here wrecks the joint and they invite us back!'

There were laughs all round and even Caitlen was shaken out of her gloom by Gina's reference.

'I was a bit of a cow. I can't believe I kicked off like that.'

'Well, I think we need to concern ourselves with finding your bitcoin device,' Gina said, changing the subject to more pressing matters. 'Have you any idea where you might have dropped it?'

'I had a good think about it during my long incarceration,' Caitlen smiled, her sense of fun returning now she was back among friends. 'I thought I had it in your apartment, Gina. I have to have lost it there – I'm as sure as I can be that it wasn't lost in the street.'

'I did ask about it while I was waiting for you to be released. Nobody has handed it in to the police station, although I'm not even sure they'd know what it was if they did find it.'

'It has to have been in your apartment, Gina. Is it possible somebody could have sneaked in this morning? The door was ajar for maybe five or ten minutes.'

'I didn't see anything,' Harriet said. 'I crashed out last night after all the fuss. Emmy was asleep, too. It was only Kasey's knock at the door that woke us.'

'Wes was out early,' said Kasey, thinking through the events of the morning. 'I didn't hear him go, but I heard him come back in. He went straight to the shower. He'd been for an early morning run on the beach, I think. I guess you have to do something to stay in shape like that.'

'No, it wouldn't have been Wes, the door was only slightly ajar, he wouldn't have even been able to see it from your end of the hallway. I wonder if it was a cleaner or something like that?'

Caitlen was baffled by the incident. She kept running through that morning's events. They'd woken, had the text exchange with Kasey, taken turns to shower and gone out for breakfast. She hadn't been thinking about the contents of her bra when she placed her clothes on the sofa waiting for her turn to freshen up. It seemed improbable that anybody could have sneaked in in that time.

'Let's check your apartment and the bins and everywhere else one more time,' she said.

'Is it safe to go out into the hallway?' Gina asked Kasey.

'Yes, you're fine. Emmy and Terry went off together ... Sorry Caitlen.'

'It's alright, Kasey. Terry is the least of my problems right now. I'm almost grateful for my short spell with the police. It gave me time to clear my head. I'll try to make it as painless as possible for everybody tonight, but I think we all know it's over for me and Terry. And truth be told, I'm relieved.'

'That's good. I'm pleased you're okay,' Kasey said. 'I asked Wes to get lost for the day and he seemed happy to – he wanted to check out some more bars and see about getting work. I thought it was better if he made himself scarce, bearing in mind what happened with Becky. There are bound to be a lot of mixed-up emotions today.'

'Matt's over in my apartment now,' Harriet interjected. 'He has a sore head and looks like he's been badly beaten up. Well he has, I suppose. He's very embarrassed and humiliated by last night, but he'll survive. He and I have some serious talking to do. In fairness to Becky, we need to clear the air with her, too. It's just a horrible situation.'

'How about Naomi?' Caitlen asked, recalling the terrible words they'd exchanged.

'Rhett was seriously hungover this morning. In fact, they were the last to leave the apartments. They headed out for breakfast and then to spend the day sleeping it off on the beach.'

'So who does that leave? Becky and Porter?' Caitlen ran

through a checklist in her head. 'I'd forgotten all about poor Porter. Talk about the holiday from hell. Not only does he catch fire, his wife leaves him too. I'll look forward to reading his TripAdvisor review.'

'Talk about the odd couple,' Kasey said, laughing. 'They figured out there was nobody left, so they went off on their own. Porter didn't seem to have much trouble walking, but he did make a bit of a meal of it at first. Becky was being remarkably patient with him. They went off shopping, I think.'

'How is Becky?' Harriet asked, her cheeks colouring.

'She's more annoyed with Wes than she is with Matt. I don't know what happened between those two last night, but she seems mighty pissed off with him. I barely spoke with Wes today, he was showered and out like a shot. Maybe those big muscles conceal a tiny manhood.'

There was laughter all round. Porter and Becky were certainly an unlikely couple, but at least they'd got company for the day.

'So we're safe to come and go now until people start to gather for the meal?' Caitlen asked. 'I don't want us to run into Terry and Emmy. I know we've got to thrash it all out, but I think we both need to be prepared for it first.'

'No, Naomi, Becky, Terry and Wes are all on a warning. They've got strict instructions to text me before they enter the building. I don't want any more fights like we had last night. We're going to hammer this out before we go out, so we can make-up, have a great night out and go and get drunk. And anybody who won't behave, isn't invited. Does that sound fair enough?'

Caitlen reached up and kissed him on the cheek.

'Thanks for doing this, Kasey. All I ever wanted was for

everyone to have a lovely time together. It wasn't too much to ask, was it?'

'You and I need to speak to Terry,' Harriet said to Kasey. 'You know what about.'

'What is it?' Caitlen asked. 'Don't tell me Terry is having an affair with Kasey, too?'

'No, nothing like that,' Kasey replied, giving Harriet a stern look. 'It's nothing, Cait, honestly. Just a bit of outstanding business that Terry and I have to sort out. You don't need to worry about it – it doesn't affect you at all.'

'Okay,' Caitlen replied, not at all reassured. If Terry was so adept at hiding his affair with Emmy right under her nose, she wondered what else he'd been up to.

'So, a final search of my apartment, a look in your apartment while Terry is out, and then the last couple of hours in the sun before we all start gathering for the showdown,' said Gina.

Kasey frowned.

'Please don't call it a showdown, Gina. I prefer to think of it as a reconciliation. Please God, don't let it all kick off again. Right, you lot, buzz off. I'm going to get a table booked for this evening. Is seven o'clock alright?'

'Seven is fine,' Caitlen confirmed, looking to Harriet and Gina for approval.

The three women spent the next half hour searching high and low for Caitlen's USB device. They had no luck in either of the apartments.

'It'll turn up,' Gina reassured her, and besides, even if somebody has picked it up, they can't do anything without the passwords. At least you had the good sense to hide that from prying eyes.'

'Do you know what, Gina? I just want to forget about it for a couple of hours. I hope you girls have both been waxing regularly, because I fancy a nice sit out in the sun until it's showdown time – sorry, reconciliation time. I want to forget everything and relax for the rest of the afternoon. Are you coming or not?'

'I'm not sure about the waxing bit, but I'm on!' Harriet replied, glad of the escape. 'I'll check in on the wounded hero next door and get changed. Meet you by the pool?'

Gina walked across the hall to her apartment to get changed and Caitlen pulled the door shut behind her so she could do the same. Thankfully Kasey had thought to take the key cards from everybody as they left their apartments for the day.

Seeing Terry's clothes strewn across the bed made it feel like he was a million miles away. In her head they'd been separated for some time. It all seemed so easy now. He'd actually done her a big favour. This removed all the drama. She could make a clean break and move on. If only she could get her hands on that missing device – she could kick herself for being so careless.

There was a tap at the door, it was Gina in her bikini and Harriet in a one-piece. Being the older woman in the group, Caitlen had opted for the more modest one-piece with sarong. She had no intention of taking on her companions in a swimsuit contest.

As it turned out, she had nothing to be afraid of. There were all shapes and sizes gathered around the poolside. It did her ego the world of good. They managed to lay their hands on three sunbeds and before long they were frying in the afternoon sun, protected only by the wisdom of Gina who'd thought to bring along some sunscreen.

The chatter had long since died down and the three women were enjoying the semi-comatose state that only fierce sunshine can create. Gina was staring idly into the distance, watching the world go by and not taking notice of anything in particular as she did so.

All of a sudden she shot up on her sunbed, as if she'd been stung by a wasp.

'What is it?' asked Caitlen.

Harriet opened her eyes, but was happy to lie still and await an explanation.

'Look who's back already,' Gina said, turning to Caitlen. 'It's only Wesley, no doubt up to his old tricks. Look at all those bags. The boy's been out shopping.'

Caitlen looked ahead and checked him out. He was wearing a sun visor and shades.

'He's had a busy day. I saw him out this morning while I was walking up the hill to bail you out of Spanish prison.'

Caitlen gave Gina a pretend snarl.

'Cow!'

'It looks like he's been to the airport. He wasn't carrying that shopping bag when I saw him this morning.'

TWENTY-SEVEN

Porter and Becky: Benidorm

'HOW'S THAT leg of yours, Porter? I'm not walking too fast, am I?'

'It's better than it should be, to be honest with you. It looks sore as hell, but with the bandages and the cream on it, it's not so bad. It's when I have to change the dressing that it's most painful. Besides, I have a supply of painkillers, so I'm feeling fine.'

'I can't believe Kasey chasing us away like that,' Becky said as she offered Porter her arm. He didn't need the help, but thanked her anyway.

'I guess it's for the best,' he replied. 'I'm not sure that I'm ready to face Emmy yet. I mean, our marriage has been dead for some time. There's no hate there just – well – I think we both lost interest a long time ago. What is it they always say in the agony columns? *We've grown apart.* Well, that's us. We've just been going through the motions. I'm beginning to understand why I've been feeling so discontented.'

'Oh yes, how's that?'

Becky was intrigued. She'd never really spent any time alone with Porter. He was part of the group so she would engage with him in a general way, but she couldn't recall a time when they'd been alone together like this. She'd been a bit pissed off with Kasey because she'd rather have been with Naomi or Caitlen. It was like she'd got to pick last in a PE lesson and Porter was the only one left to join her team. However, now they were chatting for the first time, it was flowing easier than either of them had expected.

Porter changed the subject, he wasn't ready to share yet. He was inching closer towards that personal precipice. It exhilarated and frightened him. He feared that he might truly be a monster inside.

'So, what are we going to do today?'

'How about we find somewhere to sit down and admire the view? Maybe we can try some shopping later, if your leg is up to it.'

They headed towards the beachfront and walked from bar to bar, examining the menus and seeing how British they could get with their selections.

'Are you smoking still?' Becky asked. 'Do we need to find somewhere outside? They seem more relaxed about things out here.'

'Vaping, you mean,' Porter corrected her. The distinction was important to him. It allowed him one more small deception with himself. He wasn't a smoker, he was a vaper. Neither was he a killer – he was a victim of an unfortunate accident. Dr Barbara Lawrence had told him as much.

'I won't be vaping any more. I think that little incident was

God's way of telling me to quit. Besides, Emmy always said that I looked like an idiot with that thing in my mouth. She said it looked like I was giving R2D2 a blow job the way I sucked away on it. I'm beginning to wonder if she had a point.'

Becky ventured a giggle, but stifled it as quickly as it had started.

They finally settled on a bar and ordered a couple of bacon rolls and a pot of tea between them.

'We're so English when we're abroad, aren't we? Look at us, tea and a bacon roll, it's so predictable,' Becky said.

'What is it they say? *When in Rome do as the Romans do.* I say bollocks to that. When in Spain do as the English do ... just not with the rain constantly pouring down.'

'I'll second that,' said Becky laughing.

'What did you think of Wes's behaviour last night?' she asked, out of the blue.

'What, when we all fell out?'

'No, when we came back to my apartment and you came into the hallway to see who it was. Before all the others arrived and it all kicked off. When it was just us three.'

'He seemed fine. I noticed that he was very touchy-feely with you, but I figured you're a grown woman.'

'Did you think he was drunk at all? Or maybe even a bit high?'

'No, not particularly. Why?'

Porter looked at her closely, trying to figure out where she was heading. He thought back to what had happened. After returning from the hospital, Kasey had abandoned him for a night in the Old Town. He was lying on the sofa feeling sorry for himself when he heard a loud crash in the hallway beyond the apartment. At first he'd thought it was a break-in, so he stepped outside to see what was going on.

Becky was there with Wes. Her apartment was directly opposite the one that Porter and Emmy had been using. Wes had dropped his guitar case onto the marble floor, that's what had created the noise. As Porter stepped out of his door, he ran straight into him. He was kneeling on the floor picking up a pile of key cards which had evidently just dropped out of the case. Porter bent down to help.

'Oh, hi, are you alright there?'

'It's alright I can do it,' Wes snapped, then immediately softened his tone. 'Thanks Porter, sorry I disturbed you.'

'What are these?' Porter asked. They looked just like the key card he was using to access his own apartment.

'Oh ... er ... just some spares I got from reception. We've not really had enough to go around so I thought I'd ... er ... surprise Caitlen and get some extras.'

They invited Porter in for coffee – or to be more precise, Becky invited Porter over for coffee. She was concerned about him being on his own all night while everybody else was out on the town. It had been immediately obvious to Porter that Wes wanted him out of the apartment. He was usually a bit slow to pick up on the social signals, but it was clear that Wes wanted him to buzz off. The sooner, the better by the look of it.

He'd made his excuses, but not before asking Becky if everything was alright. She'd been fine – concerned about his leg, but clearly not worried about Wes's presence.

'He did something a bit weird last night. Nobody's ever done anything like that before, it was a bit of a shock.'

Porter looked at her.

'You mean weirder than being a key-card kleptomaniac?'

'No, but that was a bit odd, I agree. Fancy hanging onto all those key cards and not handing them out. Very odd.'

She took another bite of her bacon roll and chewed it slowly.

'I assumed that you two had ...' Porter began. 'I thought that you had ...'

'You thought we slept together last night, didn't you?'

'Well, I ... Well, yes. I mean, he walked out of your apartment in his underwear.'

'Jesus, Porter, what kind of slag do you think I am? I'd just broken up with Matt in the most humiliating way possible. I was looking for a shoulder to cry on and Wes seemed to fit the bill. I figured that he's a sensitive soul and all of that. You'd have to be to sing like that, right?'

Porter nodded, chastened, his face red.

'I'm sorry, I think we all assumed ... well, to be honest with you, I'd kind of forgotten about it all, what with Emmy and Terry. So, how come he was in his underwear?'

'After you left we had a heart-to-heart about what happened with Matt and he was nice. I mean, really nice. He gave me a cuddle – nothing flirty you understand – and then he played a couple of songs for me on his guitar.'

'I thought I heard music coming from somewhere – I assumed it was from one of the bars. It was just before it all kicked off outside, wasn't it? I was drifting in and out of sleep on my sofa by that time.'

'He excused himself to use the bathroom and he was gone for longer than I'd have expected, so long that I went through to the bedroom to get changed for bed. I just assumed that ... Well, you don't just go to the bathroom to pee, do you? I was thinking how pleased I was that I'd gone off with him after the row with Matt. He'd really helped to calm me down and make me feel better.'

Porter poured a second cup of tea for them both.

'So what happened?' he asked.

'I heard the lock open on the bathroom door and was thinking that it was probably time to call it a night.'

'It must have been late by then. The others came back in the small hours.'

'It was. And I was tired. When he went to the bathroom, I crashed out for a moment. I was ready for my bed, that's why I got my PJs and dressing gown on. But he stepped out of the bathroom stark naked. He was just standing there with no clothes on. The confidence of the man!'

'Oh my God, what did you do? What was he thinking?'

'He must have read my vibes all wrong because I wasn't interested at all. All I could think was how small his dick was in relation to the rest of his body. What a ridiculous thing to think of at a time like that.'

'What did you say?'

'I was saved by the bell. I was just starting to blurt out something about being very sorry if I'd given off the wrong signals when it all went crazy out in the hallway. And after that ... well, you know what happened, it all got a bit silly until Kasey banged our heads together. But what on earth would make a man I barely know do something like that? Did he really think I'd be up for it?'

'I'm sorry you had to experience that,' Porter said.

It angered him that he'd been just across the corridor. He'd been in the same room as Wes, and he'd seen what he was angling for before he took his leave. But he'd assumed that Becky was fine, that she could take care of herself. And what if they hadn't all been drawn out of their apartments by the commotion in the hallway? Would Becky have been safe with Wes?

'Do you think we ought to mention it to Caitlen?' Becky asked. 'I mean, we just took him on trust, didn't we? He seemed like a nice guy. I'm wondering if there's another side to him.'

'I think you're right, I think we should speak to her about it tonight. It's a tricky one to broach because she's paying the bills and it was Caitlen who let him tag along. We should tell her and give her the chance to make her own decision.'

'There's another thing, too. Kasey said that Wes had left early this morning so I didn't get to see him and neither did Kasey.'

'Blimey, Becky, there's more? You had one heck of a night last night. What else happened?'

'I might be wrong, because I was tired. I crashed out when I got back to the apartment last night. But ... I might have been imagining it. I've been asking myself all morning if I led him on in any way, so I'm seriously doubting myself at the moment.'

'What is it? Don't blame yourself for what Wes did, that's totally on him.'

'Thank you, Porter. I need to hear that right now. It's just that ... when he was in the bathroom, I don't think he was only getting undressed in there. He could have done that much faster. When I went to the bathroom first thing this morning, my phone was in there.'

'Maybe you left it--'

'No Porter, I'm not sure about a lot of things that happened last night, but I do know I'm not imagining this. He'd been looking at my phone. He'd been going through the photographs. I'd been stupid enough to tell him about something bad that I'd done and I think he was looking for something in particular. I'm sure he has Caitlen's passwords.'

TWENTY-EIGHT

Benidorm: June

'I CAN'T BELIEVE IT. Brotherhood of Man! What are the chances of them playing here while we're visiting?'

Naomi had calmed down considerably. A day lying on the beach, walking around the market stalls, enjoying some soft drinks in the beachfront bars had been exactly what she needed. Rhett was thankful for the respite too. He knew they were in deep shit financially, but it was their deep shit. Caitlen had no obligation to dig them out of their hole, even if it would have been the most helpful thing she could do.

It was a long time since he and Naomi had just chilled. It was good to park their problems and enjoy the sunshine and relaxed atmosphere.

'It's very cloak and dagger, Kasey keeping us all apart like this. I mean, we could have shared a minibus and saved some cash. It's a bit wasteful coming up here in dribs and drabs.'

'It's the best thing, if you ask me. I'm going to apologise

to Cait. I've been a cow. Kasey did the right thing giving us time to think things over.'

The plan had been made and Kasey had played a blinder. He'd arranged a meal at Benidorm Palace and there was entertainment laid on afterwards. They'd all have to behave in public and they were under strict instructions to be civil with each other. After a day spent apart, they'd had plenty of time to do some thinking.

It was like a military operation, but there was no messing with Kasey. He had the whole thing planned. He'd booked the taxis and figured out who would be arriving and when. He'd paid for everything out of his own pocket. Caitlen told him she was grateful for that, it was a thoughtful gesture.

First to arrive were Caitlen, Harriet, Matt and Gina. Their trepidation at the forthcoming awkwardness was immediately tempered by the sight of the venue.

'Wow! Benidorm Palace, just look at it! It's all sparkly and showbiz, I love it!'

Caitlen had never been anywhere like it before. It was a cross between Las Vegas glitz and a bingo hall. Everywhere were posters, mirrors and bright lights. The main hall was lined with dining tables all positioned around a huge stage. There were bars at either side and smartly dressed serving staff whizzed along the aisles, darting between the tables and serving food to the assembled crowd.

There was an excited hubbub and many people had dressed up for a night out. A waiter showed them to their table. They'd pushed the smaller tables together so that they could sit in a group, and Kasey had paid for bottles of Prosecco to be placed in ice buckets to greet them when they arrived.

'Did you see how that waiter was looking at you?' Harriet said to Matt.

'Well, he does look like he's gone three rounds in a boxing match!' Caitlen teased.

Matt was still looking rough after the trials of the previous night, but he and Harriet had worked through their difficult conversation already. He knew he was wrong, he should never have taken refuge in Becky's arms after their break-up and now he owed Becky a huge apology. She'd get it too, no reservations. But he and Harriet were staying together. They'd keep it cool at first, he'd respect what she'd told him about her past. It felt just like it should have been: Matt and Harriet back in their rightful place.

Naomi and Rhett, accompanied by Porter and Wes, were next to turn up. Caitlen noticed how Kasey had carefully staggered the seriousness of the disagreements. She and Naomi were first to deal with their awkwardness, Kasey was giving her a dry run before Terry arrived. The next taxi was the one that could really make or break the evening. It was a powder keg on four wheels: Terry, Emmy and Becky. Kasey would travel with them too, just to make sure things remained civil and controlled for as long as possible.

Naomi rushed directly up to Caitlen and without saying a word pulled her in close and began to cry.

'I'm so sorry, Cait. I said some horrible things. I really didn't mean them.'

Caitlen cried too, relieved that this would pass over as just another sisterly spat. It was a bad fight, and there were wounds to be healed, but Caitlen knew that so long as they were still talking they'd work it out the way they always had.

'I need to tell you something, Cait,' Naomi said, when she finally pulled herself away from her sister. 'I haven't been honest with you. Rhett and I are in trouble. It's why I've been such a cow about your money. Let's not do it now, but we need to talk – this evening if we can. I don't want to hide this any longer.'

'We will, we've got the whole night ahead of us. Just let me get Terry out the way first – I need to make sure that we can be civil together.'

Rhett gave Naomi a kiss on the cheek and put his arm around her waist, steering her towards the table. Porter was hovering close by, anxious to get a word in. He was about to sidle up to Caitlen when her attention turned completely. The final party had entered the room and were making their way along the aisle with Kasey leading the way.

'Here we go!' Caitlen muttered under her breath. They'd all had time to think about it. They'd played it through in their minds several times that day. Caitlen made straight for Terry, took his hand and suggested that they go and talk at the bar.

Porter, who had now forgotten what he wanted to say to Caitlen, was looking at Emmy, seeking a clear signal as to how it was going to play out. They sat at an empty table to the side of the main group and began to talk.

Becky was initially more concerned about Matt's bruises than she was about thrashing out their differences. She was terse with Harriet – that was only to be expected – but they were polite to each other. Matt suggested they take a walk outside, away from the others.

Kasey dismissed the waitress, requesting an extra half hour before they ordered food.

'We'll just get drinks in for now, and start on the Prosecco,' he said, surveying who was left of the group: Harriet, Gina, Wes, Rhett and Naomi. He did a quick run-through in his head. As far as he was aware, there were no ongoing tensions between this small group, they ought to be safe for twenty minutes or so before the others started coming back.

He pulled up a chair next to Wes, just as Gina came over to join them.

'Good evening, Wes, nice to see you still here. No guitar this evening, I see. Not planning to go up on stage and steal the show from Brotherhood of Man then?'

TWENTY-NINE

Benidorm: June

WHEN CAITLEN WOKE the next morning, it took her a little while to recall the events of the night before.

It had been a good night, she remembered that much. She'd actually felt some sympathy for Terry in the end. They were equally to blame. And he was no worse than her – she had slept with Luke, after all. In spite of what she'd told herself, it really didn't make that much difference if she'd cheated once or a hundred times. The simple truth was, neither of them was happy in the relationship and they hadn't been for some time. The money had rocked the boat, but they both agreed it had needed rocking.

'We should have ended it ages ago, Terry. It was fun for a while, but it never should have carried on. We're both to blame for that. I hope things work out with Emmy, really I do.'

Terry had been unusually subdued, as if he had things on his mind. There were no wisecracks, no attempts to gloss over what was going on. Caitlen wondered if he had hidden depths. She doubted it, this was no time to be romanticising Terry.

'What about the money?' he asked.

'What about it?'

Caitlen had thought they'd got through the worst of that night, but maybe there was more to come.

'I had this in my pocket. It's yours, isn't it?'

Terry was holding her USB drive.

'Oh thank God, Terry! How did you find that?'

'I was going to throw it away. It got mixed up in the clothes that were on the floor when ... well, you know, when you walked in on me and Emmy.'

'I thought I'd lost it! Damn, Terry. I can't tell you how pleased I am that you've found it. Gina and I were going spare trying to work out where it was.'

She took the USB drive, placed it in her pocket and gave Terry a huge hug.

'Looks like somebody has made up!' Kasey observed as Caitlen and Terry returned to the table.

'Look what Terry had!' Caitlen said, mainly to Gina. 'He had the USB drive. It got mixed up with his clothes last night. He's had it in his pocket all day – no wonder we couldn't find it.'

'You'd best keep it safe from now on,' Kasey said.

'Well, it was in my bra until last night and it's staying in my pocket tonight. Gina, let's get it safely stored in one of those secure mailboxes tomorrow. I can't take the strain of carrying it around with me all the time.'

Caitlen lay in bed thinking through the events of the previous evening. She looked over at the bedside table. Where was she? It was Gina's apartment – they'd made up the spare room. That's why she didn't recognise it.

All things considered, the night had gone as well as could be expected. Porter and Emmy had as good as come to the same conclusion as she and Terry. Neither of them was happy in their marriage, it was time to move on. Things were tense, understandably, but life would continue. They'd get to the end of the holiday and try to figure things out. It was an opportunity for change.

Matt and Becky were last to rejoin the main group. Becky looked fraught and upset, but they had clearly succeeded in making their peace. She even managed an uncomfortable and awkward hug with Harriet.

'It's as good as we're going to get,' Kasey had whispered to Caitlen. 'I think we might just about get through this evening without any murders.'

Caitlen replayed the rest of the night in her head. Damn the metal shutters on Gina's apartment windows, it made the room so dark. Caitlen couldn't tell if it was an only hour after she'd gone to bed or if she'd been sleeping for the past two days. She hadn't a clue what time of day it was.

She thought back to the meal. The food had been good, and when Brotherhood of Man had come on stage the whole room had gone wild. They'd had an amazing time enjoying all of the hits from the 70s. So why did she still have an uneasy feeling about the night before?

There were some strange things going on, that's probably why. Wes looked like he'd got food poisoning; the easy charm had left him and he seemed uncomfortable and agitated. She'd seen both Porter and Becky having words with him, but the music was so loud she couldn't catch what they were saying. She'd had a brief conversation with Wes – he seemed very interested in her bitcoin story – but it wasn't long before Gina intervened and encouraged him to move on.

Terry and Kasey disappeared while the band was on. Harriet was involved somehow, but she didn't go with them. She was urging Kasey to do something or other, but she stayed with Matt, claiming her territory as if she didn't quite believe that Becky was off the scene.

Naomi appeared to have something weighing on her mind as well, but she was too fast with the Prosecco and tipsy before they'd even finished the meal. It had been a strange evening. All of their issues were supposed to have been tackled, yet she had a lingering feeling that there was still unfinished business.

Caitlen's phone began to vibrate. She switched on the bedside light. Damn, why had she set the alarm so early? She searched her brain, wondering why on earth she'd even set it in the first place. Then she remembered. That was the other part of her conversation with Wes. He'd asked her if she wanted to take the walk up to Benidorm Cross the next morning. Everybody had been talking about it at some point during the holiday. She'd been a bit tipsy at the time, but had agreed to meet him up there after his run. The night had gone well and she was feeling a bit groggy. A walk up to Benidorm Cross to meet up with Wes was just the thing she needed to clear her head.

EPILOGUE

Benidorm: July

'I'D FORGOTTEN what a climb this is,' Caitlen laughed. 'I must have been half-drunk still when I came up the first time.'

She stopped and Gina followed her cue. She took Caitlen's hand and squeezed it.

'It's okay, it's going to take some time before you get used to it. A lot has happened in the past month. Your life has taken a complete turn.'

'I'm thinking ... I came up here that first time ... I hadn't any idea the body was there. It was just in front of me in the bushes. I honestly had no idea. I'm thinking of him lying there ...'

'Are you sure you still want to do this? We can go back down if you want to?'

'No, I want to do it. I need to get up there again. If I'm going to be buying a villa out here, I need to get over it. I'm not to blame for any of this. I'd rather it hadn't happened the way it did, but ... well, he was playing with fire.'

They sat on one of the large concrete blocks that lined the road. It was definitely not a climb to complete without regular breaks, particularly in that heat.

'Are you ready to speak about it yet? I thought it might help coming up here. I can barely believe what happened.'

Caitlen's phone cheeped and she took it out of her back pocket.

'It's Luke. He says he'll be over at the weekend. The paperwork is all sorted and he's got a place to stay.'

'You're not moving in together then? I assumed ...'

'No, it's a bit soon for that. After Terry I thought it would be better to get to know each other again first. I don't want to repeat that mistake. We've decided to play it cool and see if we still have as much in common as we used to. I think it'll be okay – but once bitten and all that!'

'What do you think will happen to Terry?'

'Can you believe it? A bent copper! And with Kasey too. I hadn't got a clue what he was up to. He's been suspended, of course. And it looks like they'll prosecute. Stupid idiot, what on earth was he thinking? At least it'll all work out well for Kasey. Poor guy, he must have been scared as hell all these years. Who would have thought? I just accepted him as a friend, I never even thought about visas and all that stuff.

'It's a complicated issue. It's dead easy in Europe, but when you get into the US, life's less straightforward. Are you ready to move on?'

Caitlen stood up, took a swig from her water bottle and continued the long climb up the winding road.

'I can't believe what a bunch of fools we all turned out

to be. I wonder what would have happened if I'd never found the money on my computer. Would we have carried on oblivious to it all? Or does money bring out the worst in us?'

'I think it just accentuates existing traits. Terry was on the take before he found out you had money. He was already doing it in a small way. And as for Wes--'

'It's so hot out here in summer, I can see why everybody goes crazy over air conditioning.'

Caitlen changed the subject. She wasn't ready to talk about Wes. Not until they reached the top.

'Anyhow, I'm going to help Kasey with his legal fees. Harriet reckons that he'll be able to stay. Nobody needs to know about the forged identity; the visa issue should be sortable.'

'Good. I liked Kasey. He was about the only member of the group who didn't have a row with anybody.'

Caitlen smiled.

'I think you're right. This walk felt a lot easier when I came up here that morning. I was thinking about it when Luke's text came through. You realise that you saved my life, don't you?'

'No, how? You haven't told me this.'

'Well, it's been a crazy few weeks. But I only figured it out the other day. If it wasn't for you, it would have been my body they found up this hill.'

'We're nearly there now – this is the car park. We follow that dirt path over there and it takes us up to the Cross. Last chance. You're sure you want to do this?'

'I'm sure. Let's get it over with.'

The path to the Benidorm Cross was marked by a wooden fence. A steady flow of tourists were coming and going, and in the car park were three cars.

'Just look at that view!' Gina said. 'It never gets stale – this is the way to see Benidorm.'

Caitlen stood next to her, the breeze cooling their faces, the light glinting from the sparkling sea forcing them to squint.

'The body was over there, by those bushes,' Caitlen suddenly said.

'What, beyond the fence?'

'Yes, a dog found it. Some woman who lives at the bottom of the hill walks her dog here in the mornings. The police were already here when I arrived.'

'How come you got so lucky then? Have they worked it out now?'

'Yes, they got a confession. I still can't believe it. Wes told me he'd meet me up here and that he'd be out for his run first. I fully expected to see him here waiting for me, but instead I found a crime scene.'

'I still don't understand how I saved you. I was snoring away in the next room and I didn't even hear you leave the apartment that morning. As it turns out, me and Prosecco don't mix well.'

'That's just it. I remembered that Wes and I had agreed to meet at the Cross, then go for breakfast afterwards. Nobody else wanted to join us, so we agreed to go alone. Fuck 'em, I thought. I'm going up to the top of that bloody hill if it kills me. I didn't want to miss this amazing view.'

'I wish I'd come with you. I'm sorry I was out cold.'

'But Gina, you saved my life. When you changed the clock on my phone to Spanish time – the day I got taken away by the police after wrecking that bar – it made me an hour late to my meeting with Wes. I couldn't work out how I'd messed up the time, but I got up here sixty minutes after I was supposed to. When my alarm went off I rolled over and went back to sleep. I figured it was UK time and that I still had an hour to play with, silly cow that I am.'

'Bloody hell, I thought I was doing you a favour when I set your clock properly, but I didn't realise I'd saved your life. So he was waiting up there for you?'

'Yes, he thought it was just me and him, but that's not how it played out.'

'Porter?'

'Yes, Porter. He'd been trying to get my attention all night to tell me something about Wes, but with all the distractions going on he never got a chance. Once Naomi started spilling out her heart about their debt problems, I kind of got waylaid.'

'How are Rhett and Naomi?'

'The insurance company agreed to cover their fine as they'd been with them for so many years. They got lucky, if you ask me. And I've bailed them out on their mortgage arrears. I've no wish to see them down on their luck. She should have told me sooner. Rhett managed to win back an old contract, so it's early days, but they don't have to work in that burger bar any more. I think they'll recover, and I've told them I'll help them if they get into trouble again.'

'And Porter?'

'Not great. He's undergoing psychiatric assessments, but it's not looking good for him. I went to see him, you know. To thank him. If he hadn't done what he did, however misguided, we wouldn't be here now. I feel so sorry for him. He's clearly a troubled man.'

'So he was waiting for Wes all the time?'

'Yes, he walked ahead, even with that bandaged leg of his, so he could watch out for me. How kind is that? He was hiding in the bushes, he just wanted to make sure Wes wasn't up to anything. You know Wes had got hold of my passwords, don't you?'

'From Becky's phone?'

'That's right. She emailed me and told me what was going on. She's been to see Porter too. It seems she has some mental health issues of her own. I should have guessed – we've seen glimpses. But Becky's alright, I'll keep in touch. She's even ended up using Porter's psychologist.'

'How did Porter do it?' Gina asked.

'Porter had walked up here to confront Wes, if he was up to no good. He was planning to lurk in the bushes and make sure I was okay when we met up. It turns out Porter's had some personal issues that he's been dealing with for years – the suspected murder of his own brother. They're looking at the case again now this has happened. He admitted it all. He reckons he's had a compelling urge to kill all this time. Who would have thought it? Porter, the man whose arse caught fire at Erin's Bar!'

They burst out laughing.

'Poor Porter,' Gina said. 'I'll never forget looking at him and watching that smoke coming off his trousers. He did you a big favour. I never warmed to Wes, he was a chancer. I take it he worked out that if he had the codes all he had to do was get his hands on your USB drive and he was good to go.'

'Yes, remember we saw him with the airport bag? He'd already got his flight booked. I don't think he'd figured out how he was going to do it, but when Stupid here told everybody that Terry had found the USB drive with all the money on it, he hatched his plot. As you say, he's a chancer. He got the passwords from Becky's phone and I'd told him where the USB drive was. The police think he was planning to take the USB from me and do a runner on the next plane.'

'Would he have killed you for it?'

'It's highly likely. Will we ever know? Porter says Wes had a knife with him, but they haven't recovered it yet. That's what made Porter strike him with that rock. He says he saw Wes handling the knife and the anger got the better of him. Just like that. There's an investigation going on about something that involves Wes in the resort he was staying in when he was in Thailand. They think he may be connected with a woman who was found strangled. I think things just got the better of Porter when he saw Wes all alone up there. And you heard how he behaved with Becky. Wrong place, wrong time for Wes, I think.'

'You don't think Porter would have ... if you'd been on your own?'

'No. No chance. I asked him that when I visited him at the psychiatric unit. It was Wes he wanted, not me. It was never me. He was angry with Wes.'

'What a group you are!' Gina said, taking Caitlen's hand. 'I'll bet Benidorm has never seen anything like it!'

'I doubt that,' Caitlen replied, 'but what a carry-on. And I thought we'd all have a lovely, relaxing break out here. How wrong was I?'

'You're a wealthy woman now and I'm very pleased for you. I'm even more pleased that we'll be going into business together. I know there have been better starts, but welcome to Benidorm!'

Caitlen gave Gina a hug and looked out across the sea towards Peacock Island.

'None of this would have happened if I hadn't found that bitcoin on my old computer. I'd thought we were all friends, but look how we were all at each other's throats in no time at all. It just shows that when it comes to money you never know who to trust.'

AUTHOR NOTES

I was originally going to write a completely different book from *Friends Who Lie*, then in December 2017 I went to Spain on holiday with my son, saw lots of great locations, and came back with a strong idea for a story which I couldn't resist writing straightaway.

Most of the action in *Friends Who Lie* takes place in Benidorm. Now, if you have read any of my thrillers you will know that I have a soft spot for Spain, particularly the area down the coast from Alicante, which includes Benidorm and Torrevieja.

Benidorm is full of British pubs and eating places and the Brits have flocked there for years to enjoy the Spanish sunshine and the beautiful beaches.

I tend to go out in the winter, it's too busy and too hot for me in the summer. But even in the winter, when the resort is packed with retired people from all over the world, Benidorm is just a great place to be – there's so much to see and do.

This book is directly based upon my experiences during my visit, and if you head over to my website at https://paulteague.co.uk you will find a picture gallery showing some of the key locations featured in my story.

I hesitated about making it bitcoin that Caitlen discovered on her computer, but I needed something that could create incredible wealth for her completely out of the blue. Essentially, I needed a plot device which could drive a wedge through a group of friends and bitcoin seem to be a modern way of doing just that.

At the time I went to Benidorm I had just got interested in cryptocurrencies and was learning about how they were kept safe and secure, but also how vulnerable they could be.

I was wary of getting too bogged down in explaining what bitcoin is or where it is stored and how it's protected. Hopefully I managed to convey the key points without turning it into a bitcoin user manual.

I also think that you're going to see cases quite like this in the future as people discover that they've bought and perhaps lost considerable amounts of money dealing in cryptocurrencies.

I often feel when I'm writing my thrillers that these are as much books about relationships as they are tense whodunits. Caitlen's relationship is pretty messed up, as are some of the other characters in the book.

Most of them have something to hide, and that doesn't necessarily make them bad people. As with most of the characters in my books, they're just flawed in a very human way.

With Matt and Harriet I was keen to explore the type of relationship that just won't die, when two people are compelled to be with each other in spite of the world conspiring to pull them apart.

In Caitlen's case she's just fallen into a relationship with the wrong guy and she can't figure out how she's going to escape and can't face the drama of doing so.

We've probably all known people like that at some time, and if you've been in situations similar to these the solution often seems so simple yet at the same time impossible.

With Rhett and Naomi it really is a case of keeping up appearances. They're in deep trouble. Rhett did something wrong but not unforgivable, and they are just trying to keep their heads above water. At the same time they're incredibly embarrassed by the situation and don't want anybody else to know about it.

I wanted to make Gina a likeable character to come into Caitlen's life, one who offered her the possibility of a different future. We've all been at stages in our lives where we're not happy and sometimes daydreaming about change can be intoxicating to us. Gina represents that possibility of change in Caitlen's life, the breath of fresh air that she so desperately craves. By the way, she makes a brief appearance in my standalone novel, Two Years After.

You'll notice that I like to have a few little digs about things that I observe in everyday life and this time it's people who smoke e-cigarettes who come off worse. Poor old Porter and his exploding cigarette! However, my books are not there to make political points. I just wanted to set Porter up for a scene which I hope made you laugh.

The karaoke scenes are based upon my own experiences in Magaluf when I first tried my hand at it in a bar on the island. My wife and I were sitting next to a British couple and, although our partners were not the slightest bit interested in having a go, the other lady and I were keen to try our hand, so we performed a duet of 'You're The One That I Want'. I was terrible, but she was great – getting up to perform a song with me gave her courage and she was away on her own after that. I think karaoke is a hilarious gift to mankind, and of course some people are excellent at it, but I wanted to bring that sense of fun to this book.

This story is unusual for me since the murder takes place on the first page and the resolution pretty well occurs on the last page. The rest of the book explores the pasts, the jealousies and the personalities of the people who may have committed the crime. I hope you get a sense of rising tension and throughout the story you're trying to guess who it is who commits that foul murder at the Benidorm Cross.

I've walked up to the Benidorm Cross on a hot day and it's exactly as described in the book. The comment I made about somebody leaving the ashes of a loved one at the Cross are based on fact. There really was an urn filled with ashes placed next to the Cross when I visited.

I hope that my love of the resort comes over clearly in this book. If you haven't been there, you really should give it a try. If, like me, you prefer a quieter holiday I suggest you pop over during the winter months. However, if you like nightlife and quite a raucous environment, then summer is the best time for you to visit.

If you've enjoyed reading my thrillers I'd be delighted to hear from you, and if you've got tales of Benidorm to share, then all the better!

I send out occasional emails to my readers with details of my latest books and what I'm up to as an author. I'd love you to sign up and then drop me a line in reply to my welcome email to let me know what you're reading at the moment. Just head over to my website at https://paul-teague.net/thrillers.

I look forward to hearing from you very soon!

Paul Teague

DEAD OF NIGHT PREVIEW

Sunday 00:23

There was a heavy thud against the bonnet of the car. Something – or someone – had emerged from the woodland, out of the fog and the darkness, onto the road in front of them.

Lucy cried out, abruptly woken from her doze.

'What the hell was that?'

It was late and, bored of chatting through the day's events with Jack, she'd been half asleep.

'Shit!' he cursed, slamming on the brakes. The car swerved onto the muddy verge. They veered too far to the left, running into a shallow ditch, the wing striking a tree. Whatever it was, it had shattered the glass of the windscreen and Jack had lost what little visibility he'd had.

'That must have been a deer. It was huge.'

Jack pulled on the handbrake and put the gear stick into neutral. As if it mattered, they weren't going anywhere.

'What lights have we got in this bloody thing?'

He scanned the control panel of the car looking for the

interior light. Damn hire cars, he could never find the right switch without fiddling around for five minutes. It was cheaper to hire than it was to get the clutch changed in theirs. When he found the light switch they gasped as they saw what was splashed across the windscreen. Blood. A lot of it.

Lucy began to panic.

'Look at the mess on the window. What would do that?'

'Keep calm, Luce. I'm going out to take a look. You coming?'

'No thanks, I'll stay here. Put the headlights on full beam, you won't be able to see a thing out there. Take your phone too, you can use the torch.'

'Good idea,' said Jack, retrieving his phone from the glove compartment and opening the door.

'Christ, it's cold! Pass me my top, will you?'

Lucy reached over to grab his tracksuit top from the back seat. It was still wet. She handed it to him and then felt her ankle to see if her sprain from earlier was any better. It had been some run. They'd both done well to finish. And now it was a long drive home in the dead of night. They wanted to get back for Hamish, to be there before he woke up

'Be careful out there. It's muddy.'

'No phone signal,' Jack said as he stepped out of the car and looked at his screen. 'The car is fucked. This thing is going on a tow truck. Who knows where the nearest phone box will be, if there even is one ...'

His voice trailed off as he moved to the front of the car.

'Don't you think you should close your door?' Lucy called after him, but he didn't hear her. She tried to lean over to close it herself, but she felt a twinge of pain in her leg. A half-marathon, the first in quite some time too. Of course she was aching all over.

Jack continued to inspect the damage to the car. Lucy lowered her window as he came round to update her.

'It was big and heavy, whatever it was. There's blood on the bumper and all over the bonnet. It's made a right mess of the front. You did remove the insurance excess when you booked the car, didn't you?'

'Yes, it's fine, there's no excess. We can blame the bump in the car park on this too. It'll be less embarrassing than admitting we didn't see that low wall.'

'There's something moving over there. Please don't tell me it's still alive. I don't want to have to finish it off.'

'Is there a wheel wrench in the boot?' Lucy suggested. 'You could kill it with that. Is it cruelty to animals if you put something out of its misery?'

'Press that button next to your knee and open up the boot. I'll see if there's anything heavy in there. I can't see a bloody thing in this fog.'

Jack walked off, holding his phone out for light, for what little good it did him. Lucy gently stretched her legs, testing for pain and strains. She was stiff, but everything was moving fine. Carefully she eased herself out of the car. It was on a slope and she was getting out into a low ditch. As she took her weight on her injured ankle she became more confident realising that nothing seemed to be too badly damaged. She leant back into the footwell, fumbled around for the boot switch and heard the click as it opened. Jack was cursing several feet away. They might be needing that wrench.

Jack appeared out of the gloom. She saw the light from his phone first, then the fluorescent strips on his top. He was pale with shock, she couldn't remember when she'd seen him look like that. She immediately knew it wasn't good.

'What happened? What is it?'

Jack lurched to the side and threw up onto the muddy verge.

'It's a man,' he said, wiping his mouth with a tissue. 'We hit a man.'

'Oh, my God. Is he alive?'

'He's alive. I don't know what to do. He's barely conscious. Can you get a phone signal? Is there a first aid kit in the car?'

'Damn it, Jack. Where did he come from? We're in the middle of nowhere. How can we hit a man out here?'

'Check your phone, Luce, see if we can get some help.'

'No signal. Nothing. My battery's almost gone too. Where is he? You haven't left him in the road, have you?'

'What else could I do?'

There was a feeble moan up ahead.

They turned and walked to the front of the car.

'Jesus Christ, Jack.'

Lucy surveyed the bloody mess on the road. It was a man, forties she thought, his dark hair was greying. He wasn't dressed for the outdoors, he looked like he'd just left the office. He was wearing a shirt, no tie, and dark trousers. His right eye was blackened and bruised, his face scratched and bleeding. His leg was bent back awkwardly, exactly as he'd fallen after being struck. Bone was sticking through his torn trouser leg. His thick glasses were damaged.

This time it was Lucy who threw up. She'd seen things like that on TV, but with a real person lying there, crying with pain, it got the better of her. She wiped her face, as Jack had done, and walked back over to him to try and figure out what to do next. She struck something with her foot and knelt down to inspect it. It hadn't felt like a stone or a stick. It was the man's wallet. She picked it up, they'd need it for identification when help came.

'What shall we do?' Jack asked. 'I don't know whether we should move him or leave him here. We might do more harm than good if we carry him to the car.'

'What's your name?' Lucy asked, finding the courage to bend down and get closer to the man. He was struggling not to pass out, muttering urgently. She put her hands on his head to try to make him more comfortable, but he flinched.

'Careful, Lucy, he might have broken his spine. We can't just move him, we'll need to get some help.

'What the fuck am I supposed to do? He's in pain, he could be dying. I wasn't the dickhead who hit him anyway!'

And there it was again. Her rage could surface at a moment's notice.

'Look, Luce, we're going to have to go for help. One of us will have to stay with him. We'll need to find the emergency triangle in the back of the car and set up some sort of cordon or warning in case another car comes along the road. There's nothing else we can do.'

She knew that he was right. And it made sense for her to stay with the man. Her ankle was not as bad as she'd thought it was, but who knew how far it was to the next village? Jack would have to go.

'You get off, try and find some help. I'll make it as safe as I can here. Put your running bib on, you'll light up better if any cars come. In fact, get mine out of the car too, it'll make us both more visible.'

In silence they put on the safety gear that they'd used during the race only hours before. Jack moved to kiss Lucy, but she was in no mood for it.

'Be as fast as you can, Jack. I don't want to be left alone here with him.'

He touched her arm and jogged off into the thickening fog. The man became agitated. At first Lucy thought it was the pain, but he was desperately trying to get her attention.

'What? What is it? What's the matter?'

She leant in closer, his voice was so weak.

'Run ...' he said, his hand reaching up to hold her arm, 'run ... for your life!'

From nowhere came headlights on full beam, a vehicle revving hard, speeding towards them. Lucy flung herself out of the way. It struck the man, spinning his body with the force of the blow. Lucy gasped.

'Jack!' she screamed, but he didn't hear her, he was too far along the road.

The vehicle stopped beyond their own car, and she heard the change of gears as it started to reverse. The passenger door opened. She saw a hand, it was holding something. It was a gun. She saw the light as it fired, the bullet hitting the injured man's head, its impact spattering her with blood.

Lucy watched as the shooter fired a second bullet into the body and then levelled up his weapon to aim at her. She'd seen all she needed to. Still clutching the wallet, she turned towards the trees and did exactly what the man had told her to do.

She was running for her life.

Dead of Night is available as a paperback.

ALSO BY PAUL J. TEAGUE

Don't Tell Meg Trilogy

Book 1 - Don't Tell Meg

Book 2 - The Murder Place

Book 3 - The Forgotten Children

Standalone Thrillers

Dead of Night

One Last Chance

No More Secrets

So Many Lies

Two Years After

Now You See Her

Morecambe Bay Trilogy

Book 1 - Left For Dead

Book 2 - Circle of Lies

Book 3 - Truth Be Told

ABOUT THE AUTHOR

Hi, I'm Paul Teague, the author of the Don't Tell Meg trilogy as well as several other standalone psychological thrillers such as One Last Chance, Dead of Night and No More Secrets.

I'm a former broadcaster and journalist with the BBC, but I have also worked as a primary school teacher, a disc jockey, a shopkeeper, a waiter and a sales rep.

I've read thrillers all my life, starting with Enid Blyton's Famous Five series as a child, then graduating to James Hadley Chase, Harlan Coben, Linwood Barclay and Mark Edwards.

If you love those authors then you'll like my thrillers too.

Let's get connected!
https://paulteague.co.uk
paul@paulteague.com

Printed in Poland
by Amazon Fulfillment
Poland Sp. z o.o., Wrocław